EYE OF THE STORM

LORDS OF ARCADIA
BOOK TWO

JOHN GOODE

Published by
Harmony Ink Press
5032 Capital Circle SW
Ste 2, PMB# 279
Tallahassee, FL 32305-7886
USA
publisher@harmonyinkpress.com
http://harmonyinkpress.com

Eye of the Storm
Lords of Arcadia: Book Two

Cover Art by Paul Richmond
http://www.paulrichmondstudio.com

ISBN: 978-1-62380-054-3

Printed in the United States of America
First Edition
October 2012

eBook edition available
eBook ISBN: 978-1-62380-055-0

PRELUDE

"Travel between the realms is, at best, a tricky endeavor.
If one has to make such a journey, he or she should use the
established Facilitation Points set up by the
Arcane Council during the Time of Enlightenment.
To ignore this basic requirement is akin to suicide, since
traveling outside the recognized points involves traversing
The Nowhere."
Encyclopedia Arcadia

NOWHERE is a nebulous concept.

By the very definition of the word, Nowhere describes an absence of a place rather than the presence of an actual location. Nowhere is generally believed to be a place holder, a something with no actual value. A verbal zero, you might say.

The dictionary definition says it is not in or at any place. To be no place or not at all.

That definition was coined by people without real knowledge of the universe because, if they knew the truth, they wouldn't sleep well at night. Anyone who knows the truth sleeps with at least one eye open.

There exists between the realms a sliver of space and time that is so thin and yet so infinite that any attempts to measure it are useless. In the halls of Arcane Academies all over the nine realms, there are stories whispered in the dead of night, tales told to Initiates about those lost in a Sending gone awry. They are the equivalent of mystical urban legends, stories of people no longer here and no longer there, people who are no longer anywhere. There is nothing more terrifying than the thought of being eternally stranded in a place that doesn't and yet somehow does exist.

What most people don't know is that Nowhere is a very real place, a place where the rules as we understand them do not apply. A piece of unreality where light is the absence of dark, life the absence of death, and concepts like good and decency do not exist. Everyone who travels from one world to another unFacilitated must in one way or another deal with The Nowhere.

Some have attempted to map The Nowhere, but none who have tried have returned from the journey intact. Some staggered back, minds shattered. Others returned as husks of the people they had been before they had left. Most never returned, lost forever in their wanderings. The dark tales rose from those and other such tragic stories. The ones who were still able to speak talked of things once glimpsed that are never forgotten, things that sit and wait.

Kane doesn't know these stories.

He will have no idea about how close Ruber's spell came to not working. He will never have a clue how much the energies they were chasing had dwindled as they bolted through the portal. And most especially he will not know that he came out of the spell only by the merest thread of providence.

What Kane will remember is that he has seen a realm that mortals are not meant to see, and because they aren't meant to be where he traveled, there are simply no words to describe it. His mind will struggle with the concept that the darkness was alive and that the screams he had heard were actually appendages of a much larger creature. He will try to define the smell that permeated his clothes as something other than hungry blood but ultimately fail. And only after a long while will he forget the feeling in the infinite pause that something moved in the distance toward him, a predator slithering at its prey. In his dreams he will struggle with the certainty that, in that lapse, he locked eyes with a Something he couldn't name….

And that the Something stared back at him.

To summarize: one moment Kane was on Earth and the next he wasn't. Anywhere.

Kane felt himself falling with a velocity that was as terrifying as it was impossible. In one breath he was Kane going after Hawk. In the time between his inhalation and—but there was no "and." There was only not—no sound of his heart beating, no warmth or cold on his skin, only the dim awareness that he was hurtling at hundreds of miles an hour through The Nowhere and had no control whatsoever. There was no wind rushing against him, no whistling of air past his ears, just his uncontrolled attempts at movement and a wild panic that he had made a terrible mistake. He barely had time for his mind to register anything consciously before he was roughly ejected back to normal space just as he exhaled.

The only prelude to his appearance in the snow-covered lands was a shimmer in the air like heat coming off a desert floor and warping the air above it, and the sound of sizzling as the cold air was superheated in an instant. Kane dropped like a rock into the clouds of steam and plummeted into a snowbank. His body was numb for some seconds, his brain unable to make his body react to any of its commands. Kane's exposure to The Nowhere and then to being buried in snow created a powerful numbness that his ragged nerve endings could not comprehend. Within two breaths, his benumbed limbs began to tingle as invisible needles of icy cold cut into his skin. He suddenly jolted back to life, screaming as his body and mind recovered from the effects of the spell and forced his mind to realize he was freezing to death.

His eyes burned as he breathed in ice water and coughed some of it out. He thrashed in the snow, panicking as he struggled to come to terms with his situation. He knew nothing but pain and fear as he half inhaled another mouthful of snowmelt. He tried to scream again and was rewarded with another mouthful of ice. Kane was drowning and there was nothing he could do about it. His struggles began to slow as his brain, already tested nearly to the breaking point, screamed for oxygen. His mind locked up as the agony that was surrounding him began to fade.

Kane's next-to-last thought was an apology to Hawk for failing him.

His last thought was that this was not how he wanted to die.

That was when the air around him exploded.

CHAPTER ONE

"The Frigus are easily the hardiest of the twelve tribes that make up the indigenous population of the Articus. Unlike their brethren, they do not leave the lands during the deepest cold. Instead they remain and watch for signs that their savior Logos has returned to them."
People and Places of Northern Arcadia
3rd edition

FERRA EBONMANE was cold.

That sensation was nothing new; the people of North Frigus were used to the intense cold. They lived off a land that was locked in a permanent state of frost. They, like the other eleven barbarian tribes of the North, had become adapted to the colder climate, so much so that their skin had taken on a light blue hue as if already half frozen. They were considered by outsiders to be a hardy people who thrived on the frozen plains of Articus, a land that was as unforgiving as the people who lived there. Survival was not a certainty; every day was a battle against the elements and their deadly embrace. And that was the way the Frigus liked it.

Well, most of them liked it.

Ferra Ebonmane did not like it one iota.

She hated the cold in the same way she was sure that the cold hated her back. Ferra was sure the land did not like her people, that it resented their presence so far north, and that the Articus winds took every chance to remind them of that animosity. The frigid winds and frostbound land were a constant enemy in her mind, a silent and patient foe that waited endlessly in the high grass for a Frigus to falter.

They lived too close to the Facilitation Point that led to Niflgard, the realm of water and ice. That proximity made the cold this far north more intense than those in the lower plains experienced. But the cold was more than just a matter of temperature; it provided a major impetus for the Frigan state of mind. At best they were considered by traders, travelers, and the other northern peoples to be an unfriendly bunch. At worst they were downright hostile to outsiders. Even the most rugged traders dealt with the Frigus quickly and during the early daylight hours, knowing that no offer of shelter over the night would be forthcoming. That was the way it had always been and the way it most likely would always be.

If Ferra had had her way, the small settlement's population would travel south at the first sign of late High-Sun season frost. The other eleven tribes made the trek to warmer lands for the very same reason, and they seemed to exist just fine. Why her people had never adopted the practice, she would never know. That's not true—she knew why they stayed. She simply did not believe the same as they did.

They waited in this godforsaken cold for their savior to return to them here in what they considered the promised land. He was referred to as the Ever-Living Man, but his name was Logos. The tales told that he had sacrificed himself for their well-being eons ago and ascended to the higher planes. Those same tales spoke that one day he would return and gather the faithful to him as the world was ending. Logos would reach down and pluck his children free as The End drew near. He would take them with him to the higher planes where they would live for all eternity in blissful peace and perfection.

Of course, that was only if you followed the strict set of rules left behind by those who had walked with Logos to his death.

She paced the circular stone-paved floor of her karmak, struggling to keep herself warm. Mindless and ferocious, the wind howled against the thick mammoth hide that made up the roof of her house. Although drafts spiraled under the tightly bound and chinked edges, the sturdy Frigus-house stood undamaged. Small vents carefully constructed to allow circulation without damage to the structure were part of every karmak.

Thoughts worried at Ferra like eddying drafts of the storm wind. There had been no indications of the oncoming weather. In fact, the Elders had promised fair skies three days before. Everyone had been caught unprepared. Storms of this intensity were rare even for the Far Articusica, and this one had overtaken them out of nowhere. Living near the Niflgard Facilitation Point, the Frigus were accustomed to violent storms that blasted in on swift winds and swirled out again as quickly. They were a byproduct of living where they did, and it was a curse they had learned to bear with a quiet dignity. Normally, there was nothing to do but to hunker down and wait for the snow and wind to pass, but this storm was different. It seemed as if it would never end. Karmaks were built below ground, large swatches of earth dug out with roofs made of leather to cut the wind shear down to a minimum. Because of their construction, karmaks conserved as much heat as was physically possible, but the intensity of the wind and cold left precious little heat for Ferra's comfort.

She hated facing an enemy she couldn't put her hands on.

Dying in combat would at least be a fitting end. Defending her home and lands against an enemy was an honorable death, and she didn't fear the idea. But to have her people swept from the face of Faerth by snow and ice while huddling in the ground was just too disgusting a fate. She watched her roof shift again against the charging wind and narrowed her eyes in anger. All she asked was a way for her to grasp the cold with her two hands so she could strangle it to death.

Seconds later she heard the shouts from above.

Four men stood guard at any given time during the night. The Frigus had learned the hard way that the wildest of storms was no defense against the predators that stalked the night this far north. Hunger drove normally skittish creatures to madness, a fact that the Frigus had learned centuries before. Since her people were seminomadic, they had no concept of a graveyard, a place to bury and visit the dead. Instead, fallen people were burned and their ashes were rubbed into the thick leather hides that made up the roofs.

Every roof was black as night.

The word of Logos referred to the using of magic as "The Wicked Arts." It was said their power came from a dark place, a place where He Who Shall Not Burn resided. Because of this, only the Elders were allowed to practice The Arts, and even then only in the name of self-preservation. Each night they gave the four guards wards against the cold so they could stand guard and repel any creature that wandered into the camp as they slept. Though Ferra could not grasp the concept of any living thing venturing out in a storm such as this, the cries of the guards spurred her to instant action. Grabbing her spear, she climbed the two earthen stairs to the hatch of the karmak. During a lull in the howling wind, she rolled enough of the hide off its frame to allow her egress. She could make out the forms of several people already running past her karmak.

As soon as she rolled down the door skin, pounded it back into the frame, and stood up, the wind blasted her from behind, cold cutting through her furs as if she were naked. She ground her teeth in anger, certain that the cold was taunting her and her inability to defend herself. Ishia half ran, half blew to a stop beside her, his young face flushed with excitement. "What is it?" he shouted at her eagerly.

He was barely fourteen long suns, still at the age when everything was an adventure, no matter how dire the situation might be. Ferra had found over the years that the only way to tolerate any male with a desire to prove himself to others was to simply treat him as any other eager pup and slap him down firmly and swiftly.

"Are you under the impression that I possess some kind of advanced ability of perception that you are lacking?" she snapped at him. The younger man shrank away from her, maintaining his distance as they jogged toward the commotion at the edge of camp. He seemed to consider responding to her words, but the look on her face made him quickly—and wisely—reject the possibility.

Most of the tribe huddled on the very perimeter of their camp. Any comments they might have made were swallowed by the gale. Ferra pushed her way through the crowd and stared. It became pretty obvious what had attracted the guards' attention.

Ten feet away from her, a circle of ground over twenty feet in circumference and completely devoid of snow and ice still steamed a little. In the center sprawled an unconscious youth who was in no way dressed properly for even the lightest of their cold. Next to him, a large ruby lay half buried in the ground. Its usual color barely showed through the black charring; the gem appeared to have been grabbed from a great fire. Whatever had deposited circle, youth, and gem could not have been natural. The edges of the circle were perfectly scribed, although the snow had begun making inroads immediately.

The air stank of magic and, from the way the Elders were whispering and gesturing, there was more going on than normal vision could see. Her people were distrustful of The Arts; even the minor powers the shamans possessed were enough to make them outcasts in their own tribe. The Frigus valued their stability, and anything unusual was looked upon as something negative.

No one moved as they all wondered what to do next. And the boy continued to freeze.

ATER watched as the nyxies held their hands over Hawk's wound.

Their entire chamber seemed to be alive as the greenish glow that emanated from the walls cast their shadows against the far wall. He wasn't easily spooked, but the sisters' mere presence was dangerously close to spoiling his inner calm.

The two dark elves had taken the boy directly to The Under, avoiding any and all stray glances that may have recognized the heir to the throne. Pullus had carried the young prince, a concerned look on his face, as they rushed through the underground warrens that made up the home of the Dark. They both knew a clutch of nyxies had made their home deep in the earth near the entry to The Under. The nyxies' ability to heal was Hawk's only chance of survival.

Ater had never trusted the strange gray creatures and, up to that moment, had never been as close to them. He watched as the center creature paused the faint motions of her withered hand over Hawk's wound before she turned her face toward the two elves. "He is dying."

Ater tried not to shudder. Unasked for, the nyxie's words sounded in his head as if they had been spoken aloud, even though the old woman's mouth remained closed. Nyxies were empathic vampires, living on the emotional residue generated by other beings. Any strong emotion—sorrow, pain, fear—was food to them, so they often lived near large collections of sentient minds. Most of the time they remained hidden away, since their appearances were disturbing even by the bizarre standards of the Dark.

Their skin was the color apathy and indifference would be if they were expressed with color, a flat gray that was the very opposite of what living flesh should look like. It was impossible to tell if there was any difference among the three sisters since their hair, a long and tangled mess of white with the consistency of heavy yarn, curtained their features as they peered down at Hawk. But all of that could be overlooked in a place such as The Under. However, the creatures' eyes, or, more correctly, their lack of eyes, could not be ignored. Not that their eyes had been removed; they had never existed. Where a pair of eyeballs should have been, two slits of skin folded into the empty sockets, magnifying the absence rather than concealing it. Yet the creatures gave no indication they were blind. They moved with no hesitation or hindrance wherever they went, which made most wonder under hushed breath about what they truly did or did not perceive.

"I know that," the dark elf replied, trying to keep the exasperation out of his voice. "That is why we brought him to you three." The other two nyxies had not stopped their constant hovering over the wound and peered up toward their eldest sister and the Outsiders. Their expressions were those of hungry scavengers who had stumbled across a freshly discarded kill. The image did not do anything to further Ater's confidence in the trio.

There was a murmur of voices, like a gaggle of gossiping women in the back of both elves' minds, as the three nyxies conversed among themselves. Ater could almost make out the different voices, though the words were veiled from him. From the look on Pullus's face, he and his mate were hearing the same thing.

After about half a minute of debate, the center nyxie looked back at him. "Take his pain? Yes. Heal his wound? In time. To do it rapidly? Impossible."

A sense that the creature was lying carried underneath its words, but since the words were sent mentally, Ater couldn't pin the feeling down reliably. Rather than argue and waste more of what time Hawk had left, he asked, "How long?" his voice openly wary.

Another burst of whispered words and then one of the other two called out, "Five days!"

Pure instinct resulted in Ater's instant comeback. "Two."

"Four!" the nyxie countered.

So there is room to bargain, Pullus thought.

"Three and no more." Ater got the sense that the job could be done in a much shorter time, but the women wished to draw the experience out. He shuddered as he considered the reasons why.

"Deal," the main nyxie said, moving toward him. She extended her hand for a handshake to complete the contract, and he could see the hanging folds of skin that fell off her palm. Gingerly he grasped her hand and could feel the touch of her mind to his as they made a pact. They would feast on the boy's pain, but their word was inviolate. He nodded as she withdrew her thoughts from his own.

"We shall return in three days. His safety—" he began.

"He is safe here; this is a place of healing," the nyxie intoned.

Ater had to concede the point. As grim and eerie as the nyxies and their lair were, most creatures in the Dark relied on the sisters for their healing. The only nonfairies allowed to attend The Academy were indentured servants of noble families. Access by the poor and The Under dwellers to an actual Mender was limited to the point of impossibility. Though the nyxie trio were generally given a wide berth because of their peculiarities, no one would ever think about causing them harm or endangering their patients. The need for their healing abilities was too great.

"It takes them three days to heal a wound?" Pullus asked him in a whisper.

Ater shook his head almost imperceptibly. "From her thoughts, the healing takes less than six hours. They want three days for *that*," he said, nodding toward the other two nyxies. They both clung to the prince's neck. Briefly, Pullus was reminded of leeches feeding on a victim. The two dark elves could only see the backs of the nyxies' heads, and that was more than enough to unnerve them. Waves of color passed through their hair, transforming it momentarily from stringy, wool-like mops into silky, luxurious strands of dark-green hair. They could see the nyxies' skin begin to lighten until the gray was a pale skin tone.

The eldest nyxie glided toward them, shooing them out of the lair. "Our deal is done. Three days, no sooner."

Ater and Pullus allowed her to maneuver them out of the area, since neither one of them wanted to continue watching the spectacle. She paused at the threshold of their cave, her withered hands gripping the curtain that served as their door. Ater turned and stopped her from closing it for a moment. "You do know who he is?" he asked, after making sure there was no one close enough to hear.

Her voice was sharp and clear as she stared eyelessly at him. "The proclivity of you mind-dead races to name everything you see is not something we've ever cared about. I know who he is because I have tasted his mind. Whatever labels you have for him are of no interest to us."

Ater noticed that she had not directly answered his question, but he had a feeling it might be the closest he was going to get to one. "Three days," he answered after a moment of thought.

She closed the curtain in his face without another word.

The two assassins walked away slowly. The masses of people who were crowded into the marketplace parted without glancing at them. Their night-black uniforms with the royal mark on their chests advertised them as royal emissaries. That fact alone cloaked them in an aura of power, which was only multiplied by the fact that dark elves were some of the most feared of the peoples of the Dark. "Do you think we can trust them?" Pullus asked as they paused at a food stand to look over the selection of roots and fungus.

Ater searched through the roots and shrugged. "We don't have much choice at this point. If we take him to a Mender, word will get back to Puck, and we instantly lose our only bargaining chip. These two," he told the farmer, handing him a brass coin in payment.

"And what are we bargaining for exactly?" Pullus asked as Ater handed him the bigger root. Their fingers touched for a moment and both of them smiled. Abruptly, Ater cleared his throat and answered, although he never lost contact with Pullus.

"We were tasked to kill the Heir and bring back the secret of ascension. Those two things we did not do. If Puck knew where the prince was hidden, how long would you estimate our life expectancy to be?"

Pullus took a bite as he considered the question. The hand that didn't hold the root shifted until his and Ater's fingers entwined between them. "The changeling is not someone who takes bad news well." They turned and strolled (as much as any dark elf was capable of strolling) toward the edge of the square. The thought of Puck's reaction quelled Ater's appetite.

Ater sighed as he handed what was left of his root to an elderly beggar as they left the square. "Oh, he is the very model of understanding. The only chance of survival we have is to convince him that we may still be able to gain the information—if our heads stay on our shoulders, that is."

"Have you considered just killing the prince?" Pullus asked as they paused outside the gate of the tunnel leading back to the surface. A passerby might have thought them only deep in conversation. Another dark elf would have known that Ater and Pullus had taken the time to sweep the area and ensure that their comings and goings had gone unremarked. Before he replied, Ater led them into the tunnel.

"More times than I care to admit," he said as he leaned against the tunnel wall.

"You do realize that, given Puck's mercurial mood changes, there is a greater than average chance he will still kill us."

Ater did know this but hadn't felt the need to vocalize it. Turning to his partner he had to ask. "Do you want to kill the boy?"

Pullus's golden eyes would seem flat and unreadable to anyone else, but Ater could see the depth of the emotion in them. He knew Pullus as he had never known any other living being, and that knowledge came from literally hundreds of years of partnership. Ater felt the roughness of the other man's palm as he placed it against his cheek in an uncharacteristic show of emotion. "As always, I follow you."

Ater leaned his face into Pullus's palm, pressing it between his face and shoulder, drawing strength from the touch. He was weary. There had been too many killings, too many deaths on his hands. When he was younger, the job had seemed so noble, defending the realm from enemies both in the realm and outside. Acerbus had angered him precisely because Ater could see himself as he'd been in his youth in Acerbus's every action. He was no longer as naive as he once had been. With the sudden shift in power, with the Dark struggling to gain some poorly defined form of recognition, the shape of things had blurred, and killing to protect no longer seemed as enticing. When Pullus's lips touched his, he started and then pulled the other elf close, stunned at the openness of his partner's concern and love. When they parted, Ater saw a faint smile on Pullus's lips and smiled in return.

"We could always run," Ater said after a few quiet moments.

Pullus gave him a wry grin as he arched one eyebrow in question.

"You're right," he said, standing up again. He grabbed Pullus's hand and squeezed it. "We've never run before, why start now?" Pullus said nothing as he leaned into him. The two of them embraced each other and stood unmoving for a very long time.

WHEN I started to wake up, I wondered why Dad had the damn air conditioner on so low. I bundled up in the covers and tried to go back to sleep, but the cold wouldn't let me. I was about to scream downstairs for him to turn up the heat when it hit me.

Hawk.

I woke up in what looked like a pit dug in the ground with some kind of teepee thing that was trying to pass as a roof. I say trying because the way the wind was howling outside, that roof could have been made of brick and steel and I would have wondered about its structural integrity. I was covered in a mass of furs, actual furs. Not fur coats, not a furry blanket, but real, honest to God pieces of dead skin that I knew without a doubt were once the outsides of actual animals. I wasn't sure how to handle that little bit of information, since they were the only thing between me being just cold and me being a Kanesicle, so I had very little room to complain.

If I were back home, I would have been brought up on war crimes for being cloaked in dead animal skins. If Hawk's leather jacket would have gotten dirty looks, what lay over me now would have condemned me as being a serial killer. A warm one, but a serial killer nonetheless.

Of course the fact that I was covered by dead animal skins took a distant second to the fact I had no freaking idea where the hell I was. Or where Hawk was—*Hawk*—and my brain stopped right at the thought of him for I don't know how long. Finally, though, I realized the only way to go to Hawk was to leave here. Wherever here was. With Ruber. Ruber? Ruber! I felt under the skins and looked around the pit thing, increasingly confused.

I had no idea how much time had passed since Ruber had cast his spell or where I had landed other than being buried under smelly animal pelts. Coupled with the fact that I had no idea where Ruber was made my first waking moments an exercise in confusion morphing into full-blown panic. I sat up quickly and the furs slid off me, which made me regret my little gesture something fierce.

The cold was a physical force crashing against my body almost instantly. I started shivering uncontrollably, and I felt daggers of ice cut into my chest when I inhaled. I leaned down, going after the furs, but my fingers were unable to grab them off the ground. Within a breath, I followed the furs.

I rolled off the bed and slammed onto the unforgiving surface with a muffled thud. The ground was frigid, which doubled the pain of impact. No breath. I was wracked with spasms as the last dregs of warmth were sapped from my body. I tried to keep my mouth clenched tight so I didn't cut my tongue in half and choke on my blood during the final few seconds of my life.

The last image I thought I saw before I passed out was that of a huge Viking woman with blue skin charging at me, screaming some unintelligible language that I wished I understood because she sounded like she was on about something. Fuzzily, I hoped that Valkyrie Smurf wasn't mad at me.

AFTER the paleskin almost killed himself, Ferra decided to sit with him as he slept.

A small drink of calor water brought warmth back to the boy, but its effects would fade quickly, leaving him vulnerable to the elements all over again.

The Elders were examining the gem that had been found with him. The faintest traces of writing of some sort were still visible at its core so it had to have been enchanted at one point, but nothing could tell them if there were any magic left in the rock now. They still had no idea where the traveler had come from. Some believed him an Offworlder due to his strange clothes and the melted circle where he'd been found. Ferra wasn't sure yet because of the blade he had worn on his hip.

She recognized it as a Soul Blade, a weapon that was only crafted by the dwarves located in the bowels of the capital city of Arcadia. Soul

Blades were reserved for the royal family and their vassals. The boy was not royalty, that much was clear, and if he was related in any way to the throne, she'd eat her boots. He looked like a vagrant, but the pack he had with him was enchanted and the ruby alone was valuable enough to buy him a small castle in some places. How he came to possess a blade whose ownership was limited to maybe a dozen beings on the planet was the puzzle, and she knew the answer wasn't going to be simple.

Which wasn't, she added mentally, good news for the boy. If her people were anything, they were simple. No, not that; they were direct and uncomplicated. Their lives were complicated enough by the fight for survival; the few times they encountered puzzles, their reactions had been almost universally violent in nature. As one does not fight in a burning building, it was equally true that, when freezing, the best decisions were reached quickly and without remorse. The boy was an Outsider and they had no means to feed or clothe him. That left the Elders precious few options to explore. The only thing that had deterred them from killing him immediately was the mystery surrounding his origins. Vagrant he might be, but he also had in his possession things that should have belonged to royalty. The Elders could only speculate. And not kill the boy. Yet.

Once who he was and where he'd come from were determined, Ferra knew the most obvious thing to do, at least in the minds of the Elders, would be to kill the boy outright or leave him to fend for himself. Either way, she realized, it would have been a mercy if he had died on the plains where he had first landed.

CHAPTER TWO

"The Dark is the collective name given
the subspecies that inhabit Faerth alongside
the humanoids that rule. Though most
are intelligent and possess their own cultures, they
are widely considered second-class citizens and are employed
doing menial work. This arrangement frees the Arcadian
people to pursue other goals such as ruling over the Dark."
Badger's Treatise on Arcadian Society
(Included in The Willow's Guide to Other Realms
and Why You Should Not Travel to Them)

THE sea of creatures surrounding the castle worked themselves up into a renewed frenzy late in the day.

Thousands of beings ranging in size from the massive ogres that stood at a minimum of ten feet tall to the diminutive grigs who were barely larger than a full-grown sparrow had amassed at the gates. Their voices were raised in anger outside the solid crystal walls that protected the capital. Each group screamed in its native language, engulfing the entire area in an unintelligible cacophony. To the untrained observer, the gathering was a chaotic throwing-together with no organization or order to guide it.

But Puck knew better.

The ogres were placed in the rear so they could watch over the surrounding area in case anyone inside tried to make a run for it. There were about three dozen Trow spread throughout the crowd—their small, misshapen forms cloaked by their innate power of invisibility—so they could eavesdrop on conversations, monitoring the mood and general demeanor of the crowd in case morale began to drop and talk of reconciliation reared its ugly head. Four crow spirits were posted at the cardinal points around the city at all times, redirecting the ley lines around the castle, effectively cutting off the flow of magic to the royal family. The rest of the rabble were brought out in shifts from The Under to rally against the walls, ensuring the royal guard would think about nothing beyond keeping the walls safe.

Puck loved it when a plan came together.

He quickly spotted Trias in the crowd, his lanky, wooden form easily visible over the tops of the shorter creatures' heads. Trias looked as if a willow tree had pulled its roots out of the ground and begun walking around. His head was crowned with long, spindly branches covered in tiny leaves. Puck had no problem navigating through the mob at all; in his natural form, he was well known to everyone who huddled on the ground, and they parted for him as if he were royalty. Though they had no idea how much of the current revolution was his doing, as an emissary for the royal family he was the closest the Dark had to a celebrity. In fact, he was the only nonfairy allowed to live in the palace, so he was widely considered the poster child for the equality movement.

"What is going on?" Puck demanded as soon as he was within earshot of Trias.

The matchstick man barely glanced down at the belligerent changeling as he leaned over the table, examining the parchment unrolled on it. He was deep in conversation with a rather tired-looking brownie who nodded rapidly every few seconds. "If the burrowers are too close to the surface, the displacement will cause a visible trail in the ground above. Make sure the gnomes stay at the prescribed depth until they are well under the walls."

A high-pitched, rapid burst of sound came from the brownie that was indecipherable as separate words. "Thegoblinsrefusetofollowthe machinesbecausetheysaytheydontcleanupaftergnomes."

Puck had no idea what the stream of sound meant, but obviously Trias did. "Tell the goblins their job is to make sure the tunnels are clear of debris. If they continue to argue, remind them there are more than enough gremlins to take their places."

"Butgremlinscantworkaroundgnomemachines," the brownie pointed out after a second.

The bark that made up Trias's face cracked slightly as he smiled. "The goblins don't know that."

Puck saw the smaller creature's face brighten with a grin before it vanished in a burst of speed. The matchstick man rolled up the map as he addressed Puck. "Good morrow, trickster. I pray you bring good news."

"What was that?" Puck asked, gesturing toward the departed brownie.

Trias explained, "The gnome machines can burrow through the earth with relative ease, but the gnomes themselves seem incapable of keeping them level. We need them close enough to burst through the ground in case of invasion, yet deep enough so as not to leave a trail that's visible from the watchtowers."

When it was obvious the matchstick man wasn't going to continue, the changeling prompted him. "And?"

The wood elemental looked over to him as he tucked the map away. "And the machines were designed to dig, not dig in a straight line. They have to be reminded from time to time. Along with the fact the goblins don't want to have anything to do with gnomes, it's been a day."

"But they are in position?" Puck asked.

Trias paused as he examined Puck, his expression critical. "What is the word from the royal family?"

Puck felt an angry retort begin to form in his mind, but reminded himself that the plan was too close to fruition for him to lose his composure. Instead, he gave the other creature a sympathetic look as he explained. "Not good, I'm afraid. It is taking everything I have to keep them from attacking so far."

"Of course it is," Trias replied wearily. "Perhaps if we stopped being so aggressive?"

Puck shook his head quickly. "The masses are the only thing keeping them from attacking as it is!" he explained. "If you were to disperse everyone, the royal family's vengeance would be swift—"

Trias held up a leafed hand to stop him. "I understand the rest of that sentence, thank you." The elemental sighed as he looked out across the teeming collection of creatures and considered his next move. "It seems we have no choice but to move forward."

"They are fairies!" Puck said, stepping next to the sentient tree. "You know they would kill us all if they had the chance." His voice was syrupy and cloying as he pushed his will against the matchstick man's mind. "This is your only choice."

"Only choice," Trias repeated, his voice becoming unfocused.

"You must kill them before they kill you," Puck said, standing right beside the elemental.

"Kill them," he repeated.

"I will lull them into a false sense of security," Puck continued. "Trust me, trust me like you trust no one else."

"I trust you like no one else," Trias echoed as if in a dream state.

Puck snapped his fingers and began talking again in a conversational tone. "It is taking everything I have to keep them from attacking so far."

Trias's response was completely opposite to his previous dismissive words. Though the wood that made up his body didn't lend itself to emotional expressiveness, it was fairly obvious to see his newfound panic on his face. "I will make sure the tunnelers are in place!"

Puck nodded, making sure not to smile. "And I will endeavor to keep the family as reined in as I can." He was pleased to see the grateful look in the matchstick man's eyes. "But I don't know how long I can hold them off, my friend. Get your people in place."

Trias put his branches together and leaned forward slightly, his people's way of expressing respect to another. "It will be done."

Satisfied he had sown the proper seeds, Puck made his way back toward the castle walls that surrounded the capital. The afternoon sun reflected off the crystal walls, its light causing the symbols contained within each to become illuminated. Puck's form shimmered as he changed from the overly grotesque image he used when dealing with the Dark to the exotically handsome features he possessed when within Arcadia's walls. He had rich caramel skin with a smooth head devoid of all hair. His was the very image of a sultan's child, holding himself with a silent grace that spoke of class and an upbringing that demanded respect. The guards on the wall recognized him immediately and gave him a salute. The walls parted like water as he walked through them. They were enchanted to allow safe passage for him to move in and out of the city limits, as he was an emissary.

Puck returned the salute as he made his way to the castle.

Perhaps a hundred various nobles had been stranded in the castle proper at the start of the siege. Most of them were simply influential people who liked having the royal family's ear when it came to local politics. Others were holders of official titles and responsibilities in various parts of the Realm.

The last, and fewest, were the actual bloodline of the throne. When Titania had completed the Ascension and assumed the throne as Arcadia's one true ruler, she had exactly three blood relations left alive in Faerth—two sisters and an aunt. Between those three, they had another five children, bringing the royal family to a grand total of nine. When she had agreed to join with Oberon, his father, brother, and four nephews had been brought to live at the castle. Including Hawk, this put the grand total of valid members of the royal family at seventeen.

Those same seventeen people needed to die before Puck had even a ghost of a chance at the throne.

When a leader fell under normal circumstances, the burden of the throne was given to the next legitimate blood relation. Since the Rite of Ascension was held once every thousand years and a ruler might perish before then, it was common practice for the bloodline to continue in power until the time came for a new rite. Only in the absence of any bloodline whatsoever would Puck even be considered as a viable candidate for the throne. As an agent for the royal family, he wasn't noble, either by blood or title, but he did represent them in matters of negotiations. Because of the overwhelming political turmoil that was caused every time a new ascension occurred, Puck was betting the people would follow him rather than initiating that chaos.

Plan B involved having the Dark kill most of Arcadia, at which time he would step in and save the day. He was sure the surviving populace would be more than willing at that point to elevate him.

Either way, he needed the royal family killed, and killed quickly.

As he entered the throne room, he could hear another in what had become a long series of debates about what the royal family should do next. It had been this way ever since the Dark had assaulted the capital. All the leaders of Arcadia seemed to do was talk, talk, and then talk some more to be sure. Only two official decisions had been reached and acted upon. One, Hawk had been sent away and two, Puck had been appointed emissary to negotiate with the rebellious creatures. Better to send one of the Dark's own than risking one of their precious nobles in face-to-face meetings with the rabble: Puck could hear Titania's logic, although she may not have said the words aloud.

Oberon's arrogant voice rose and fell as he performed his daily monologue for the assembled Fairies. "…no choice but to kill them. I'm not sure why we are even hesitating." Puck wondered if Oberon practiced each night, nailing down tone and inflection.

The Lord had been advocating setting the guards on the crowd since the first day of the rebellion. At first most of the Faerth dismissed his declarations as incendiary; however, as the days passed, Oberon's position was being considered more and more. Puck forced his expression to remain impassive as the Lord of Arcadia continued to advocate what was nothing less than genocide.

"How can we tolerate this? We are prisoners in our own city! We showed these creatures our kindness by allowing them to earn honest wages in our service, gave them opportunities they would not have had otherwise! And this is how they repay us?" There was more muted murmuring from the back than the last time the king had given this speech. Puck could tell he was swaying them, slowly but surely. These people were scared, but they were still fairies, and in their eyes everyone who was not them didn't count. "There is only one price to be paid for insurrection, and that is death."

"For everyone, my sire?" Puck asked conversationally in the lull after Oberon's final word. "Or just the ones outside?" Everyone's attention shifted to the changeling instantly. Puck could see Titania watching him from the throne as well. She had one eyebrow raised, which was her way of warning him that he was treading into dangerous waters. Puck gave her an almost imperceptible nod as he continued to speak. "There are literally thousands of the Dark that are not involved in the action at all; do we kill them too?"

"Of course," Oberon answered without hesitation. "They obviously cannot be trusted. Surely you do not expect me to believe that the ones outside are not being fed and sheltered by others in The Under? Most assuredly, you would not stand here and claim those not in front of the capital are not aiding those that are, in their own way? Should they not also be held accountable?"

Puck waited a few beats, as if considering the words. Inside he was seething. He had counted on being above any hint of suspicion when the royal family was slaughtered; he had planned to be far from the castle when the massacre occurred. However, looking at Oberon's haughty expression, having heard his casual decision to commit widespread murder, Puck knew he was going to kill Oberon personally when the time came. "Should we not offer mercy, for the sake of our own immortal souls if for nothing else?"

"*We* are merciful, dear Puck," Oberon responded, gesturing to the rest of the gathered fairies. "*You* are nothing of the sort." His gaze locked with the changeling's. "Your kind have no souls."

The silence that descended in the throne room was impressive considering the chamber's famous acoustic abilities. A chuckle or a gasp would have been heard instantly. It was obvious to Puck that everyone in the room was holding their breath, awaiting his response.

Luckily for the changeling and Oberon, the queen's voice was the next heard. "How did your talk with the Dark go, dear Puck?"

Very slowly, Puck tore his golden-eyed gaze away from Oberon and looked toward Titania. "Not well, my queen. They are thirsty for blood." Now the gasps of the assembled fairies were audible, and Puck knew he had their attention. "It took every iota of charm I possessed to keep them from storming the walls this very evening. I'm becoming convinced they might not be able to be swayed."

"So then why don't we attack?" Oberon demanded.

Titania gave her husband a withering glare but said aloud, "A fair question, if also impertinent."

Puck took a quick glance at the assembled crowd and knew he had them where he wanted them. "Why? *Why*?" he asked, raising his voice. "As you have been so kind as to remind me, sire, I and *my* kind have no souls. We are wanting in everything that matters to a sentient being, according to you and your several speeches on the subject."

"Your point?" Oberon asked, his icy tone making the room's temperature drop a few degrees.

"My point being," Puck answered, ignoring the royal fairy's ire, "do you not owe it to yourselves to show compassion? Do you not find yourselves burdened with the task of reasoning with these animals in an attempt to lead them to enlightenment? As the dominant force in the Realms, can any of you do any less than exhaust every avenue of mercy and compassion before turning to slaughter? If we are actually the beasts you believe, and your kind are our betters, then shouldn't you act like it?"

He ended his speech in a flourish and a deep bow. The silence in the hall was deafening. Then, perhaps twenty seconds later, the sound of one solitary pair of hands clapping was heard. Puck wasn't sure who those hands belonged to, but he thanked them mentally as another and then another joined in. Another ten seconds and the entire crowd, save Oberon, rose to its feet as Puck was surrounded by thunderous applause.

"Well said." Titania spoke over the roar. "Well said, indeed."

Puck did a slow turn to smile at everyone, reveling in the adulation. He saw Oberon glare over at him. The fairy's silent hatred was clear as day to the changeling.

"You die first, old man," Puck promised under his breath, smiling back as innocently as he could.

WHEN I woke up, Warrior Smurf sat watching me.

She wasn't as scary as I first thought, now that I had a chance to actually look at her. Her skin was a light blue, the same light blue I'd seen on CSI when someone froze to death in really cold water. Her hair was long and braided and was black but looked crazy-black against the paleness of her skin. She was tall, taller than most guys I knew, and was built like a linebacker. Back home she'd be referred to as big-boned; not that she was fat, it was just her proportions were *huge*. Her face was prettier than you'd expect, which kind of surprised me. Everything else about her seemed really butch and grrr, but her face and her eyes… they looked sad, almost.

I made an effort to push myself up slowly; every part of my body ached. My bones throbbed painfully, my muscles hurt from the inside out; I'd never known someone could ache so much. My head swam slightly as I slid my feet off the bed. The cold was bracing, but it helped me to wake up faster than I normally would have. I kept the furs close, though, because within ten seconds the chill had gone from slightly invigorating to teeth-chatteringly cold. I bundled up as well as I could while the blue-skinned woman watched me, her expression curious, maybe? I didn't know what a curious expression looked like among Blue Warrior Smurfs.

"Yeah, yeah, I'm a wimp. Get over it," I grumbled.

"Et going yrittää tappaa itsensä jälleen olet?" she asked. At least the tone seemed to be questioning.

"Say what?" I tapped my ear, thinking maybe I was in worse shape than I thought.

She cocked her head and asked, "Mitä kieltä puhutteko?"

That was when reality hit me. Ruber wasn't here.

I began looking through the bed frantically. Furs flew off as I searched for the ruby. "My friend, I mean—the rock," I said to her. With my hands, I made a shape that was about Ruber's size. "Rock! Large ruby?" I tried again.

She had risen to her feet, openly concerned, and picked the furs up as fast as I threw them down, using several to cover my shoulders. I tried to shrug them off, but she was not only taller but several times stronger than I was. With almost no effort, she finally wrapped the furs around me and held them with one hand while she pushed me back down to the bed with the other. "Oletko hullu? Melkein jäätyivät kerran jo!"

She was pretty upset. I think.

"I need to find my friend!" I said more slowly, using the tried and true idiot's way of speaking another language. Because if Warrior Smurf didn't understand English from another world, I was sure that if I just talked slower, she'd magically learn it. "My friend?" She just stared at me like I was insane, and I knew it was a lost cause. I sighed and stared hopelessly down at the floor. "I am so dead."

The "roof" opened up and another blue-skinned person peered down at us. "Hän on hereillä? Vanhimmat ovat valmiita hänelle."

Whatever he asked, she nodded once. The guy tucked the roof's flap down and went away. She looked at me, and I could swear I saw pity in her eyes. "Hyvin vieras, tämä on silloin he sanovat olet ulkopuolinen ja että olet pitäisi surmattakoon." She stood up and held her hand out to me. "Mennään tästä lisää."

I held my hand out and got up slowly. When she closed her hand around mine, the cold vanished almost instantly. I shrugged the furs off, since I was suddenly burning up under their weight. "Thank you," I said, looking at her and smiling.

She didn't smile back. "Älä katso minua noin," was all she said as we made our way out of her hole in the ground.

CHAPTER THREE

"History's most destructive spell was
Bable's Incantation of Instantaneous Translation.
Instead of facilitating frank and open discourse about
the differences people had with their foreign neighbors,
the spell only solidified the fact that each side was as intolerant
and unforgiving as the other, thereby becoming responsible for
some of the bloodiest conflicts ever recorded."
The History of The Arts and Society:
How Magic Has Ruined The Realms
Originally Published By Ignatius Doyle
Royal Historian of The River

THE ELDERS' hut was the only above-ground structure in the village.

The walls were covered in mystical runes that protected the flimsy edifice from the harsh Articus winds. There was another spell surrounding the building that made it practically invisible from more than twenty feet away. As Ferra led the boy across the village's central space, she could tell when the house became visible to him. He stopped, shocked, while she kept walking and inadvertently pulled his hand from her grasp.

He instantly regretted it.

Without her protection, the glacial chill took him down within seconds. She saw the color in his cheeks drain away even as she knelt down and made skin contact with his arm. He looked up, still shivering. "Gratias agimus tibi," he said with a smile.

"You are very stupid," she said, yanking him to his feet. "Do not do that again."

"Cum hoc facilius nugae," he answered in that strange tongue.

"And I'd suggest you don't try talking to the Elders like that either; there is more than enough evidence marking you as an outsider without you adding to it."

He shook his head and mumbled, "Hoc enim pertinet fabulam librorum semper videntur skip."

She gave him a stern look as she knocked on the door. "Shush!"

He seemed to get the meaning of that word, because he didn't answer.

"Enter, child of the ice," a deep voice from the other side invited them. Ferra forced herself not to comment that she wished she were a child of the warm and pleasant lands and instead led the boy into the house.

Ever since she was a young child, Ferra had hated stepping foot into the small building the Elders used as their meeting place. The thick, cloying smoke from the incense that was always burning made her nose sting and eyes water. However, a little stinging smoke would have been tolerable if not for the fact that the Elders came with it.

There were five of them at all times.

Always five, always men, always ancient. The blue of their skin had faded until it was the same as a pale sky on a High-Sun season's day. There were runes carved into their skin; the scars formed patterns that covered their arms and chests, making the loose skin appear to be some kind of clothing with arcane adornments.

Ferra could not tell them apart, which was always the way of the Elders. Each always seemed to know of his impending demise well before it happened and began training another tribe member months before he passed on. If those selected had been the oldest of the tribe, Ferra would not have had as much of a problem, since the older members possessed years of experience and might possibly have provided valuable insight to problems. However, each Elder's decision was as cryptic as his abilities. Once someone was chosen, he was secreted away inside the house and not seen by the others of the tribe until the Elder who had selected his replacement died.

The burial rite for the fallen Elder was the first time the new Elder appeared.

No matter the age of the person taken for training, he would emerge from the house looking exactly like the others: gray hair, bent spine, wrinkled face—every time. The knowledge each one received came at the price of part of his own mortality. And that was too high a cost as far as Ferra was concerned. The five old men stared through her as she walked the boy into the incense-shadowed room.

"You wished the paleskin," she said, moving the boy to stand in front of her. Knowing that the room was warm enough for him to survive, she began to back out.

"Wait with us, daughter of Jennia," one of the old men said.

She felt her spine stiffen at the sound of her mother's name being spoken aloud. Her hand clenched reflexively, almost crushing the boy's shoulder. "Heu quid infernum!" he protested, shaking her out of her stupor.

"Apologies," she said, relaxing her grip. She cursed herself, knowing the boy couldn't understand her, but she felt he got the general tone.

"He does not speak our tongue?" one of the Elders asked her.

"If he does, he hasn't to me," she answered, trying to mask her displeasure at the ridiculousness of the question. The old men knew damn well the boy didn't speak their language and was a foreigner, but still they were going to play out their charade.

"Can you understand us?" another of the old men asked the boy. There was a slight undertone to the question that brought chills up her spine as she realized the Elder was using The Arts, although well hidden in his words....

"Nullum et ligula verbis tu," the boy answered, unmistakable frustration in his voice.

She watched the five of them look at one another, seeing if any of them understood the words the boy had uttered. "He is neither from this nor any of the eight realms," the Elder sitting in the center declared. "Which leads one to wonder, where he is from?"

"Does that matter?" the one on the far end asked. Ferra was lightheaded from the close quarters and the heavy incense and was losing track of which Elder said what.

"Technically, no," another answered. "But shouldn't we ascertain his origin before we pass judgment?"

"You mean kill him," Ferra clarified before anyone else could open his mouth. They turned as one to stare at her, and she repeated herself. "Your judgment is going to be to kill him, correct?" No one spoke. "I just thought it would be helpful to say the word out loud."

"You have a problem, daughter of Je—?"

"Ferra," she said, cutting the Elder off. "My name is Ferra."

She saw the old man reconsider his words when he saw the look on her face. "You have a problem with that, Ferra?" the old man amended.

She shrugged and refused to rise to the bait. "You are the elders, and your word is law. Far be it from a simple warrior to try and give advice about what to do with an envoy from the Arcadian royal family. That decision is yours." The older men could tell from her tone of voice that she was purposely disrespecting them by downplaying the proper use of their title.

She carefully refused to smile as the five men began to talk among themselves.

"PUCK, a moment, please," Titania said as she walked quietly up behind the changeling.

The assembled crowd had surrounded the emissary with words of praise and encouragement while Oberon sulked in the corner, shooting him looks like daggers. Puck bowed to the royals and excused himself before following the queen out of the throne room.

"You play a dangerous game with Oberon," she said as they walked down one of the halls connecting the throne room to Oberon's and her own inner chambers.

Puck tried to suppress his grin as he answered, "He makes it so easy, my lady."

There was the barest hint of a smile as the queen opened the door to her private sitting room. "Even so, I would suggest not baiting a tiger so brazenly."

"Ah, but if one has acquired the taste of roasted tiger, then the bait is worth the price." She looked back at him with an expression that conveyed her lack of amusement. He bowed in acceptance and said in a much humbler tone, "As you wish."

She sat on her chair with a weary sigh. Within seconds a servant entered the room, carrying a tray upon which stood one shapely glass. Once she had taken the flute, Titania made a swift sweeping motion with her free hand, dismissing her chambermaid. "What I wish is irrelevant, dear friend. I am simply giving you some free advice."

Idly, she lifted the flute and stared at the exquisite engraving within the thin crystal that formed it. In the room's ambient light, Puck was able to make out the forms of two dragons dueling in the air. Titania finished the drink in one swallow and, without a second's thought, threw the glass across the room, shattering the fine crystal into a million pieces against the far wall. Puck tried not to think of how much that one glass was worth as she continued to talk. "Has there been word from Hawk and Spike?"

Puck kept his expression neutral and replied, "No, my mistress. Why do you ask?"

She sighed, looking magnificent even in distress. "No reason, I just…." Her words slowed as she stared off into nothing. "I just felt like he was closer for some reason." Puck felt the cold chill of fear wash over him as he forced himself not to panic and reveal himself until he was certain what Titania actually knew.

"I am worried about Spike as well," he lied. "But worrying is part of being parents, is it not?" He moved a step closer to her. "We worry even though they are more than capable of taking care of themselves."

She appeared to be unconvinced, and he readied himself for a demand that he contact Spike then and there. When she looked at Puck, he could see the ruler of Arcadia rather than the worried mother, and he breathed more easily. It was the ruler of Arcadia who spoke to Puck. "I can delay my husband for another two days at best. In that time, I suggest you try to convey the extent of his ire to the Dark. They face disaster if they do not end their insane rebellion." As she spoke, a servant entered the chamber and knelt to clean up the shattered crystal. Puck watched him with one eye as he nodded his understanding of her warning. "They cannot hope to win, can they?" she asked.

Puck chose his next words carefully. "I think they are simply tired, my lady, and feel they have nothing left to lose."

She arched one perfect eyebrow. "What about their very lives?"

In a solemn tone, he answered, "There are fates worse than dying, your majesty."

She was silent for a few minutes as she considered the meaning of the changeling's words. "Well then, they need to make a choice, don't they?" she finally asked. "Which fate do they desire? Because in forty-eight hours, I am allowing Oberon to take the guards and end this affair once and for all." She leaned in closer to Puck. "Do we understand each other?"

Puck felt his gaze lock with hers. "I understand," he replied, bowing.

She waved her hand at him as she leaned back in the chair. "You're dismissed."

"Thank you, ma'am," Puck said, bowing his way out of the room. As soon as he had shut the door behind himself, he turned with a growl and began stomping down the hall to his own quarters. "Death will be a mercy when this is over," he muttered under his breath as he entered his chambers.

Since he wasn't royalty, Puck didn't have servants dedicated to his comfort; the room was still dark, and he adjusted his eyes to see enough to find his way to the lamp that served as illumination. His fingers crabbed down the lamp's base, and he was fumbling for the small flint and phosphor when another hand grasped his wrist and held it motionless.

Ater's whispered words came from just behind the back of Puck's neck. "Hello, Puck. Let's talk."

THE gaggle of smelly old men was freaking me out.

One, the place reeked like I imagined a hippie's graveyard would. I mean, I had dealt with some serious incense blowback before, having lived in Athens my whole life, but this was too much. From what I could tell, Valkyrie Smurf wasn't into the smell either, so that was something. Two, all five of the old coots were glaring at me like I was gonna boost something from the candy aisle or something. I had seen that never-blinking gaze of Mordor before from the elderly, but these guys were rocking it to a whole new level. And three, I had the sinking feeling in my stomach that this whole meeting with the old guys was not going to end well for me. I don't know why; maybe it was the way my giant Smurf guard wouldn't look me directly in the eye. She looked like someone who didn't want to name the sick puppy because she knew he was just going to die.

I so did not want to be the sick puppy in this story.

After about five minutes of them chattering like old women who've been inhaling helium, they looked at me. I ignored the insane desire to check my pockets to see if any candy had fallen in by mistake. The one in the middle proclaimed, "Tiedämme kyllä can't ymmärtää meitä. Mutta meidän täytyy pyytää sinua kuitenkin."

I don't know if it was lack of sleep, nervousness, or just plain idiocy, but I giggled at the fact the guy sounded like the Swedish chef from the Muppets. From the glares, it was obvious they didn't think my reaction was appropriate. "Voitteko selittää mitä olit tekemässä tämän?"

The words made no sense. Then Crusty Old Man pulled Hawk's sword out from behind him and I freaked.

"Hey! Give that back!" I yelled as I tried to wriggle away from Red Sonya Smurf. No luck. She kept me in place with one hand like I was an infant. I struggled as hard as I could, but there was no way I could get free of her. My hands were outstretched as I kept trying to grab Truheart. I know I went from shouting to roaring words, and the old men gaped at me like I was a rabid dog tied to the porch while they stared from the sidewalk.

"That's not yours!" I screamed, every thought on getting Hawk's sword back. My vision blurred for a moment, and I blinked hard to clear the fuzzy and wavering images. I heard one of the old men gasp, surprised when the sword began to glow. The blue deepened until I could see it clearly, and I raised my right hand to catch it, knowing all the while that I looked like an idiot.

And then Truheart thudded onto my palm, hilt first. That seemed to grab their attention *real* fast.

PUCK shifted from human form to snake within a second.

Ater's arms tried to grab the reptile as it dropped to the floor. Immediately Puck changed again, green scales dulling to slate gray as the entire creature stretched and created arms and legs for itself. In thirty seconds, nine feet of furious Ettin lumbered upright, snatching Ater before he could escape. Squeezing the dark elf around his rib cage, Puck glowered icily at Pullus. "Don't," the changeling warned in a voice that sounded like it was made up of rocks rubbing together.

Ater, struggling to breathe, waved his partner off, knowing the shape-shifter wouldn't kill him without asking questions first. Or, at the very least, playing cat and mouse with his captive.

"If I were paranoid, I'd be worried about two dark elves skulking about in my room," Puck commented, not easing his grip at all.

"And if I were paranoid," Ater said in what voice he could manage, "I would have hit you with a dart coated in morpheme venom when you walked in the door."

Puck saw the skin on his arm ripple from the stone that made up an Ettin back to the golden fur of his true form. He screamed as he was forced back to his actual form against his will, the poison taking hold throughout his system and nullifying his powers for the time being.

Ater landed on his feet as Puck crashed to the ground, shaking violently while his muscles strained against the toxin. "The morpheme is a tricky little devil, isn't it?" the dark elf asked, pacing slowly around the quivering emissary. "For normal people, it causes numbness and temporary paralysis. But to shape-shifters, it's almost deadly." Puck felt his body curling up into a fetal position as every muscle contracted tighter and tighter, causing excruciating pain. "I am not one of your lapdogs," Ater continued, kneeling down next to him. "I have killed more people than you have ever seen or met. Try that again and this will be a much shorter conversation."

"Just slice his throat and be done with it," Pullus said as he closed the door.

"It's a thought," Ater answered, clearly thinking about doing as Pullus advised. "I have a feeling you don't have my best interests in mind, dear Puck." He placed a blade to the changeling's throat. "How about we try again?" In a lethally cheerful tone, he added, "Hello, Puck. Let's talk."

"Get off me," Puck demanded weakly, knowing he posed no threat to the deadly man who held the knife.

"We're fine, thank you," the First said, ignoring the changeling's words completely. "Acerbus didn't make it." Small pause. "What's that? Oh, it's okay. He went quickly, but thanks for your concern."

"Where is my son?" Puck asked, his voice barely above a whisper.

Ater stared directly into Puck's eyes. "He's dead. Isn't that what you wanted?"

Puck may have been paralyzed, but the smoldering hatred in his stare targeted Ater as if it were alive. "There is not a place in the nine worlds that you and your *partner* can hide from my—"

"Someone is coming," Pullus interrupted, putting his ear to the door.

Ater placed his hand over Puck's mouth and pulled him aside, hiding out of sight of the doorway. Pullus stepped soundlessly behind the door. Half a second later, Oberon stood on the threshold. He bellowed, "Creature, we will have—" before he noticed the room was dark and the changeling wasn't in his bed. "Puck? Are you in here?"

Ater held his breath as he waited for the lord to leave.

Puck focused his entire concentration into his left hand and willed it to move. Sweat broke out on his forehead when the door swung slowly shut behind Oberon as he left the room. Though it was unnoticeable from the rest of his body's shaking, Puck could tell his hand was shaking harder. The light from the hall was just a sliver; the door had nearly closed.

Ater felt Puck shift under him and moved, but he was already too late.

Puck's fingertips formed into a blade that lengthened swiftly when Puck's focus tightened. The dark elf felt the sharp point stab into his side and he made a small sound, reacting instinctively to the shock and pain. It wasn't loud, but it was enough for Oberon to pause. Puck felt a rush of adrenalin at his success and pushed his body, hoping the toxin had run its course. Razor-sharp quills formed around the tops of his forearm, a dozen of them drawing blood from Ater in a second. Despite his training, he cried out as he pushed himself off of the changeling.

Oberon opened the door again, his voice sharp and suspicious. "Who's in here?"

Pullus knew he had to do something. In one step he left the shadows; in the second he lunged at the Arcadian lord; and on the third, he planted his feet for leverage and raised his fist to strike home. Pullus's hope was to stun the fairy before he had time to react. If

Oberon had been a mere noble, the dark elf's plan would have been successful. Unfortunately, as Pullus discovered a heartbeat later, Oberon's leadership of the royal guard was not merely ceremonial. He drilled with them every week and his reflexes were second to none.

In this case, they were just barely second to Pullus.

The blow was partly blocked, the strike hitting Oberon's cheek instead of his temple. The lord took a half step back as he lashed a counterstrike into Pullus's solar plexus. The dark elf felt Oberon's strike knock the air out of his lungs, but he refused to let his body seize. Instead he clutched his chest and feigned collapsing to one knee. Oberon snatched the advantage and leapt forward to follow up on his attack.

Pullus lashed out with his the sole of his foot, connecting with Oberon's knee. The lord went down cursing even as the assassin rolled swiftly to his feet and drove his fist downward to the side of fairy's head. This time the strike connected and Oberon passed out instantly.

Ater stared up from the floor, his eyes wide; he could not believe what he had just seen.

"You know you're both dead," Puck croaked from the floor.

"Get up," Pullus ordered, holding his hand out to his partner.

Ater reached up, still in shock and bleeding.

"There's no place you can run," the changeling taunted, his voice echoing in their ears.

"And there is no way you can ascend without our help," Pullus retorted, guiding Ater toward the door. "Send word when you're actually ready to talk," he added before he and his partner sprinted down the hall.

"You knocked Oberon out," Ater said after a few seconds.

Pullus flashed him a full-faced grin. "It was glorious."

Ater shook his head in disbelief as they fled the castle grounds.

"NOW we're in it," Ferra muttered, taking a step away from the boy and his glowing sword.

"He raises arms against us!" one of the Elders cried, conveniently forgetting he and his partners had just threatened the boy mere seconds before. Two more Elders came to their feet as well.

"Strike him down!" the one on the far right called out as the middle one began chanting in the tongue of The Arts.

"Quod cumque facitis amet tortor!" the boy shouted above the din. "Hunc gladium demens questus!"

Again Ferra didn't understand the boy's words, but he sounded more concerned than threatening. As the glow around the Elders' hands intensified, the sword's own light matched it. She didn't know much about The Arcane, but she knew that magic begot magic and that was never a good thing. A bolt of energy flashed from one of the Elders' hands, directed at the head of the youth, who obviously had no way to counter the attack. The blade's color turned blue instantly as the bolt changed direction and went hurtling into the sword's edge.

And did absolutely nothing.

Another three arcane bolts flew and were drawn into the glowing blue metal. Ferra watched the five men grasp hands together and join their energies into one blinding light. The old men's eyes closed in concentration, repeating the simple chant until five voices merged into one, they pooled their strength. The air around her began to crackle as they drew more and more energy from ether and brought it to bear on the target of their attack.

Before they could complete their spell, the sword's hue shifted from grayish-blue to a blood-red and released four bolts from its point. The boy screamed in shock as the light daggers struck four out of the five old men, dropping them to the ground as one. The only standing Elder stopped his chanting and looked in panic at the strange boy holding the enchanted blade. From what Ferra could tell, the boy was in just about the same amount of fear and shock as well.

After a few ragged breaths, the boy called out. "Non me!"

"Non me indeed," Ferra muttered under her breath. In a louder voice she spoke to the Elder. "Maybe we should try a different approach than to kill the outsider?" The old man nodded quickly, never taking his eyes off of the sword.

She moved past the boy, keeping her hands out where he could see them. She was pretty sure he had no control over the sword's actions, but obviously it was reacting to hostile intent. She moved around the Elders' table and pulled the pack they had found with the boy from under one of the now-empty chairs. The Frigus held up the pack and showed it to him. "This is yours, correct?"

"Meum!" he declared, seeing the pack, taking a half step toward her.

"I hope that means 'Please give that to me' instead of 'I am going to strike you down with my sword of doom'," Ferra said, more to herself, edging closer to the young stranger with the pack out. With great deliberation, she reached into the bag and pulled out the only other thing they had found with him. "And this was already like this when we found it."

She handed him the cracked and blackened form of Ruber.

CHAPTER FOUR

"Reality is a lie.
Therefore altering reality is simply a matter
of telling a better story than the one already in progress."
Narghile Rhopalocera
Philosopher for the Family Crimson

HULK Smurf pulled a cracked and blackened rock out of Hawk's pack, but I had no idea what she was trying to tell me. I looked at her, confused for a moment, and she gestured with her hand again, trying to hand me the red stone.

Red?

I dropped the sword and grabbed Ruber out of her hand in a flash. Oh my God, it was Ruber! He had always been lit from within, so I had never seen him look like just another rock before. The runes that had danced within him were gone and a huge crack big enough for me to fit my fingertips into ran diagonally through him. It looked like he had been burnt from within, leaving his interior black and lifeless. I wasn't even aware I had dropped to my knees in shock until the blue woman placed her hand on my shoulder.

It was the first time she looked at me with anything besides rigid neutrality.

I had never felt so lost in my life. What a stupid thing to say. Before that moment in the smelly old men's house, the only time I had been lost was during Athens's annual Renaissance Fair. I'd wandered away from Dad during a show and then cried for ten minutes before he found me.

Oh my God, I was never going to see my dad again! I was stuck in some weird snow world with no way to talk and no idea where Hawk might be. My only friend, and my only connection to him, was gone.

I was going to die. Hawk was going to die, and Ruber was already dead.

I just cradled Ruber in my hands as I knelt there and felt myself give up. What had I been thinking, coming here? I had sacrificed my friend in a vain attempt to save my maybe-boyfriend, and all for nothing. I'd lost Ruber, I didn't have any idea where I had landed, and Hawk—*Hawk!* All I wanted to do was sit and wait for this nightmare to end.

Which lasted about thirty seconds before I realized that, nightmare or not, I wasn't waking up.

I began to examine Ruber in detail, thinking maybe I had missed something. Giving myself time to think. Ruber was the toughest thing I had ever met, and I couldn't believe he could die so easily. Maybe being back home, where magic existed, could make a difference? What if, surrounded by the ambient magic, he could start to heal… or regenerate, like a lizard growing back a limb? He was a rock, right? So maybe he could heal in the ground? I tried to dig a hole, but the dirt that formed the floor of the old men's hut was frozen, hard as stone. I needed something to dig with; there was no way my fingers were going to cut it.

I remembered the sword and set Ruber down in front of me.

Using the blade, I began to cut the packed and frozen dirt, trying not to think of how Hawk would have reacted to his sword being used like a hoe. Once I'd cracked the topmost layer, I scooped the dark, black soil out, making enough space for Ruber's body with some room to spare. I dropped the blade and picked Ruber up gingerly. I placed him in the earth and covered him with the loose dirt. Packing it down, I placed my hands over it and closed my eyes in the closest thing to prayer I knew. This had to work, it just had to. He was a magical rock, and I couldn't believe something like him could be struck down so easily.

I was also, of course, certain that jumping into a multidimensional cab and telling the driver to *follow that magic teleport* was something easy and not impossibly difficult.

The sounds of the other old men waking up just brought home how screwed I was, but I ignored them as I pressed down harder on the dirt. Hawk needed me, I needed him, and we both needed Ruber. This was not how the story ended. I didn't care how fate or God or whatever thought it should end. It was *not* ending like this.

THE rock sat in the dirt, unmoving.

Its life forces had been used to tear open a gash in time and space, to protect the insane human who'd started the whole thing, which had left it virtually defenseless against The Nowhere during the transition. There were no magical powers in the dirt and Ruber was incapable of bringing itself back to life. The scraping of soil simply provided a shallow grave for a gem elemental's body.

Nothing happened for a couple of seconds.

Which were followed by more nothing.

And then, finally, nothing.

Kane could hear the men whispering among themselves. Only a matter of seconds remained before they attacked him again. He squeezed his eyes shut even harder as he concentrated.

The rock sat in the dirt, unmoving.

The old men started to chant; Kane knew he had just let Hawk die.

The rock sat in the dirt, unmoving.

Kane thought a silent apology to Hawk and then focused on Ruber once again, much harder, even as he waited to be struck down.

When the Elders' hands began to glow, he could feel something snap inside his mind.

After that everything changed.

The rock sat in the dirt and began to absorb the magical energies contained in the soil.

FERRA heard the old men begin to chant and knew the boy was dead.

She saw the boy on his knees, helpless, praying to the hole in the ground he had dug for his blackened rock. The Frigus were a people whose entire society revolved around the challenge of surviving just one more day in the unforgiving land known as Articus. Caught between the hammer of the freezing winds and snow and the anvil of the unforgiving land, moral niceties found little room to survive. If an action or decision helped the Frigus survive, it was good. Everything else was bad. Most of the time, decisions came easily as a result.

However, Ferra thought, at times such as this moment, decisions didn't come quickly.

The laws were simple and the boy had violated them. He was an outsider, he possessed magic beyond their capacity to understand, and he had attacked the Elders. If there existed a trifecta of actions guaranteed to end in one's death, the boy had committed them. The obvious fact that he couldn't have known their laws bore no weight in the singular opinion of the Elders. And anyone helping the boy would be guilty as well. Which meant she should step aside.

But he was helpless and just sitting there.

Which, of course, made her choice that much easier.

Snatching the boy's sword up, she stepped between the Elders and the helpless young one. There was great power in the blade, so much that she switched to a two-handed grip in order to control the weapon. She could feel it vibrating in her hands as she pointed it directly at the group of old men. For a moment they didn't notice, buried deep in their spell as they were. Ferra used that flicker of time to ensure that the stranger was well out of the way and to get a better grip on the weapon. When the center Elder saw what Ferra had done, he stopped his chanting and sent her a harsh look. "Ferra! Get out of the way!"

"No," was all she answered. The single word was to be more than enough of an answer for them. Without another word or question they began chanting again, this time their target obviously her. "Whatever you are doing, boy, faster would be better!" she said over her shoulder, knowing the paleskin had no idea what she was saying.

At least the cold will be over, she thought as she braced herself for their attack.

THE energies began to knit the wounds in Ruber's body, the cracks slowly but surely mending themselves closed. When the fracture line disappeared, a small light began to pulse in the center of the ruby. The elemental's consciousness gathered itself from nothing and forced itself back into Ruber. There was no other way to put it. One second he Wasn't, the next he Was.

The ground exploded as he shot himself skyward in panic.

Images of a great void and a darkness coming toward him, flashes of light, and the feeling of a great pressure crushing him. Memories of faint sounds and more pressure.

And now he was here.

Where *here* was might very well be the question of the day.

"Ruber! Look out!" Kane shouted as the Elders launched their spells.

Five beams of light merged into one as they shot out toward the elemental. The beam shattered into an explosion of power as Ruber said in that vaguely British voice, "Protect." The glow inside him began to ramp up as he moved from defense to offense. From the way the female warrior and Elders flinched away from the display, it was obvious they had never seen anything like him before.

"Ruber, you're okay!" Kane said, standing up quickly.

"So… so I am," he said. The hesitancy in his voice was telling. Ruber always spoke with certainty bordering on arrogance. To hear him sound so lost was a little heartbreaking to Kane. "Where are we?" he asked the human after a few seconds.

"Somewhere cold," was all Kane could answer.

Since Ruber had no eyes it was hard to gauge, but Kane was pretty sure that Ruber was taking in the scene for the first time.

"The blue skin would hint we are in Articus," the gem said after a few seconds.

Kane nodded as he looked over to the warrior woman holding Hawk's sword. "And they can't understand a word I'm saying."

She cocked her head at him. "Now you can speak our language?" She seemed to sigh in exasperation. "You could have told us that earlier and saved most of this." She turned the sword around and handed it back to him hilt first, blade resting on the top of her forearm.

"Thanks, Ruber," Kane said quietly. To Ferra, he repeated, "Thank you," to which she nodded.

"Least I could do," Ruber answered, still watching the Elders. "I assume you have a plan?"

"Me?" Kane almost swallowed his tongue in shock. "Why would you assume that?"

"Because it was your choice to follow Hawk here, which means this entire adventure is on your shoulders. I am simply here to facilitate it."

"Awesome," Kane muttered under his breath. "And if these guys want to facilitate an ass kicking on us?"

"They'd find that unwise," Ruber answered with complete confidence.

"Good to know," he sighed, stepping toward the old men. "My name is Kane. We're looking—"

The center Elder didn't give him a chance to finish. "You are unwelcome here!" he screamed. "We will fight you to our last man!"

Kane stopped, more than a little confused. "Fight?" He looked at Ruber. "Say what?"

"The Frigus are notoriously xenophobic. I believe they see our presence here as an act of war," Ruber explained as if reading from an encyclopedia.

"We are not here to attack you," Kane tried to explain to the pack of old men. "Our coming here was an accident."

"You have invaded our lands, attacked us with your magics. Your intent is irrelevant," another of the old men answered. "Your actions speak the truth. Words lie."

"*You* attacked *me*!" Kane shouted. Responding to his anger, the sword in his hand began to thrum with power. "You pointed those crusty-ass yellow fingernails at me and tried to kill me with your magic missiles! It's not my fault the sword didn't like it."

Ruber concentrated on the boy, and Kane could feel the elemental's attention on him. "The sword protected you?" The boy nodded. "That is a good sign."

"We will not allow you to leave," the main Elder pronounced as if declaring the word of God to the masses.

Kane began to open his mouth, but Ruber beat him to the punch. In a tone that was the closest Kane had heard him get to anger, the ruby proclaimed, "I am the Raatnaraj Ruber Scientia, first consular to the Stone Throne and a representative of the Arcadian throne. The boy is the consort to the heir of the throne, the first prince. To touch him is to declare war on the royal family. We did not invite this aggression, but I assure you, if you continue down this path, I will personally defend the boy to the death." The jewel flashed once, and Kane could feel the energy flash past his face and slam against the warded walls. From the way the structure shook, it was obvious he could have leveled the place instantly.

"I was not referring to *my* death," Ruber clarified.

OBERON regained consciousness to find Puck bending over him.

Reacting on sheer instinct, the fairy lord kicked at the changeling as he scrambled back. Although his mind was still fuzzy about the particulars of the preceding few minutes, Oberon knew never to trust the shape-shifter. Reaching down to his boot, he pulled out a rather wicked-looking stiletto from its concealed sheath. When he saw Puck scramble to his feet, Oberon brandished the weapon. "Stay where you are!"

It was hard to gauge the creature's emotions since his face was malleable by nature, but he was rather sure Puck was sighing in exasperation.

"We were attacked. By dark elves?" Puck tried to prod Oberon's memory. "One attacked you from behind the door!"

Oberon's recollections cleared and returned to him slowly. He remembered walking into the dark room and hearing something… and then he had been struck from behind by someone. "Dark elves?" he asked, his mind catching up with the conversation. "What were they doing in *your* quarters?"

Puck cursed silently as he realized he had overshared. He could have said anyone but dark elves had attacked him from behind and been fine. But now he was going to have to explain two things. One, why the elves were in his room, and two, why they hadn't just killed them both. Seeing Oberon's suspicious glare, Puck knew his answer had better be good.

"They were trying to…," he started. "Kill me!" he added after a second. "They were sent by the Dark to kill me!" His voice gained strength as his mind commenced weaving a lie that could only serve to help him. "They threatened me to stop advocating a truce with their people." Oberon's eyes narrowed in disbelief, but Puck kept talking. "They want war, like you do! They were trying to silence the only voice of reason."

The two of them stared at each other for several seconds, neither one saying a word as they studied the other. Finally the fairy lowered his dagger and stumbled to his feet. "You must think us fools," he said, slipping the weapon into his belt. "Do you honestly believe I am not aware you are playing both sides?" Puck felt his mouth go dry as Oberon dusted himself off. "And do you think for a second I would allow you to if it didn't suit my own needs?" The sounds of guards coming down the hall grew louder, and they both knew they weren't going to be alone for long. "Challenge me again and I will expose you."

Three men barged into the room, weapons drawn. "Sire! There was a commotion…."

Oberon and Puck could see Titania hovering behind the men, her expression trying to mask her concern and failing rather badly. Ignoring the men, Oberon spoke directly to her. "We were attacked, my love; it was the Dark. Which seem to have free access to the grounds, despite the abundance of men in armor around." The guards bristled at the accusation as he continued. "They were attempting to kill our dear Puck: I was barely able to fight them off." He looked over at Puck. "Isn't that right?"

Puck said nothing for a long series of seconds before nodding slowly. "He was very valiant, mistress; I owe him my life."

"This is unacceptable," Titania said, the tone of her voice dangerous.

"I agree," Oberon said quickly. "Let me take a group of men and attack tonight."

Before she could answer, Puck stepped forward. "Before you allow that, I beg you give me one more chance to reason with them." The changeling could almost feel the anger radiating off Oberon, but he ignored it and kept talking. "They know by now that the attempt failed. If we attack tonight, they will be ready. Please, let me go and try to assure them we do not want war. Then, when they are not expecting retaliation, Lord Oberon can attack and the advantage of surprise will ensure his victory." Puck was sure Oberon wanted to argue the point, but there was no way to do so without sounding disingenuous. "If they think we are still pursuing a diplomatic option, they will be less likely to be ready for a surprise attack."

Titania looked startled. "You're now advocating an attack?"

Puck refused to look toward Oberon and just nodded. “They did try to kill me. They are obviously not honorable creatures.”

“Well said,” Oberon said under his breath. Puck continued to ignore him.

“They believe we will err on the side of caution,” Puck explained. “Let me reinforce that fallacy.”

Titania looked to her husband. “You have no objections?”

He had several thousand objections, but Oberon couldn’t voice a single one of them out loud. “If he moves quickly. I will not wait.”

“I’m gone,” Puck said, shifting to wolf form and sprinting past the guards and Titania before they could argue with him any further. He loped down the hall, past the throne room, past the nobles, and out of the castle. The people gathered at the wall were a blur of color and noise, no more. Abruptly, he left the walls behind and made his way toward Trias’s camp. Within two minutes he had reached the outskirts of the camp. A quick scan revealed the matchstick man briefing a trio of Lycans. Puck morphed back to his natural form, locked eyes with Trias, and gave his order.

“Tell the gnomes to breach now.” Puck saw Trias’s eyes widen in shock and deepened his tone until it resonated, stern and unyielding. “Go now, go right now.”

The wooden man said nothing for a full thirty seconds before turning to the three half wolves. “Send the word: we will attack within the hour.” The three boys flashed their wicked teeth as they hopped up and began to run toward the crowd. Within a few steps they were wolves, howling their excitement. “I hope you’re right,” Trias said to Puck grimly.

Puck’s mind was already miles away. “Remember, this is war. No quarter is asked…,” he began to say.

“…and none shall be given,” the matchstick man finished. “I am aware of what an attack means.” After a beat, he asked Puck, “Are you?”

The changeling said nothing as he spun and made his way toward the warrens of the Dark. The two dark elves had forced his hand and thought they had him over a barrel, but they were wrong. The changeling intended to play the hand out to its last card. Dark elves, Oberon, the lot of the Dark: all of them were going to discover very quickly that Puck played to win.

OKAY, so Ruber is kinda gangsta.

The creepy old men, who had been throwing magic bolts around like they were pickup sticks five minutes ago, were now cowering away from the furious gem-pulsar floating in front of them. From what Ruber and the blue girl had explained, these guys had a seriously anti-foreigner point of view. I mean, these blue guys made those crazy people who live on and patrol the Mexican border sound sane. They obviously wanted us gone, but Ruber made it abundantly clear he was not moving until he knew precisely where we were. It was the right world, that much he knew, but Articus lay on the very fringes of what was considered Arcadian soil, and he had never had a reason to visit here.

No matter what, a fair stretch of land lay between us and what would be considered even mildly civilized country. Most of it was filled with creatures that would look at me as an *amuse bouche* at best. There was no way the two of us could make it back without help, and there was little chance the esteemed council of Papa Smurfs was going to raise a hand for us. Which left us absolutely nowhere.

That was, until Barbarella Smurf interjected herself into the conversation.

"I'll take them."

That brought the entire discussion to a grinding halt.

Everyone stared at her, too startled to blink. "I mean it," she repeated. "I will escort them out of our lands."

The old men obviously didn't like that idea and most likely liked even less that she'd offered aloud. "These people are not our concern," the main grumpy old man shot off, glaring at all three of us. "We are not going to sacrifice one of our warriors on a task that at best has nothing to do with our people." He twisted his ugly face into an even nastier mess as he lobbed a flippant "Even one such as you" toward Barbarella.

I really thought she was going to jump over the table and slug him.

"My apologies," she said as she ground her teeth. "I must have made that sound like a request. I am taking them." From the way they all gave her death stares, that was not the politically correct thing to say.

"Um, are you sure?" I asked, making certain not to actually touch her in case she decided to go what passed as postal on this world and crush me like a grape.

She looked down at me and I saw the conviction in her eyes. "Trust me, I am sure."

The old men discussed something among them before the main guy pronounced, with the voice of doom, "Hear me, daughter of Jennia. If you leave our lands, you will not be welcome back. Ever. So make sure your choice is the one—"

"I am," she said, cutting him off and turning to Ruber. "Let me get my gear, and we can leave."

"Shall we wait here?" he asked.

She looked over at the old men and jerked her head. "They won't like it."

Ruber brightened as he responded with, "Oh, then we will certainly wait here for you."

I think that was the first time I saw her smile, and I realized she was actually quite pretty. "I'll be right back."

Ruber orientated back on the old men. "Please, take your time."

I had to admit, the old men scowling at him was funnier than it should have been.

CHAPTER FIVE

"Ever since Faerth was made the center of the Realms, more and more creatures are being discovered that have never been seen before. There is no known correlation between the two facts that I know of."
Professor Porter's Bestiary of Creatures Known and Unknown

ATER and Pullus reached the entrance of The Under and paused.

Pullus could see the healing magics of Ater's armor had closed the gashes made by Puck , but they still had to hurt. "Do you need a salve—?" he began to ask when Ater shushed him.

An unnatural silence surrounded the subterranean entrance. By that hour of the night, the entrance to the surface should have been the equivalent of lunch hour bedlam in a topside city. Their habits dictated either by genetic disposition or generations of individual preference, most inhabitants of the Dark preferred traveling to ground level under the cover of night rather than facing the unbearable light of day. Something was wrong, seriously wrong.

"Trap?" Pullus muttered.

"Puck," Ater replied, his voice cold and emotionless. Both dark elves were thinking the same thing as they studied the tunnel entrance. They had pretty much thrown down the gauntlet at Puck so they expected to face him or, more likely, the creatures he controlled, sooner or later. They weren't expecting the "sooner" to be so soon.

"He signaled ahead?" Ater asked with his hands, using the silent language of the dark elves.

"Had to," Pullus gestured back. He pointed down the bank a few feet, where a slight overhang would serve as protection for their backs. Still twenty yards above the main traffic area, they could watch without being seen. Noiselessly they crossed the distance. One quick glance behind them and they disappeared from view.

They settled in and watched both the dark entrance and the perimeter from north to south, alert to any possible movement. Seven minutes crept by and Pullus felt his dread increasing with every second that passed. Then, out of nowhere, a shaking in the weeds and low bushes below them caught their attention. No path started near that point, and nothing had entered the undergrowth on either side of it, or they would have spotted the movement earlier. Ater turned to Pullus, puzzled and uneasy. Then he heard the faint sound of a child laughing.

His hand froze in midsign.

Pullus and he stared at each other, their expressions reflecting the nearest to panic that they ever felt. Pullus signed the complex series of movements that roughly translated as "Green Children."

Green Children was the shorthand way of referring to the Woolpit Children. Half plant, half spirit, and immortal, the creatures resembled human children no older than eight years. Their green skin and hair made them almost invisible in the underbrush. Children they might appear, but children they definitely were not. Of those they hunted, none survived to tell the story, although witnesses relayed the horror. The Green Children hunted only those they were told to take, leaving witnesses and terror in their path.

Possessing no human emotions whatsoever, they were some of the Realm's most bloodthirsty killers because of their frightening lack of any compassion. Both elves knew there was no reasoning with the faunas. Once called, they could, without sleep or sustenance, wait forever for their prey to pass by. Neither Ater nor Pullus knew the secret to summoning The Children, but over the centuries their team had stumbled across the bloody remains of the Woolpit's carnage more than once. The dark elves knew the Woolpit Children were nothing they wanted to cross.

"Ideas?" Ater signed, knowing there wasn't much to do in a case like this. The Children would wait forever, and any attempt to engage them would draw more attention than either one of them were willing to risk.

Pullus signed back. "Is running still on the table?"

Ater grinned despite the seriousness of the situation.

"He wants to draw us out," Pullus added, this time far more seriously. "If he is able to capture one of us and makes us talk, it negates the prince's value."

Ater nodded, making sure not to sigh out loud. "What do we gain by pressing the attack?" he signed.

Pullus paused as he considered the options. "Nothing. We have three days before we can collect the prince," his hands flashed. "I would suggest we spend them somewhere else."

As if to accent his point, a muffled explosion from behind them shook the earth as the army of the Dark attacked the crystal wall protecting the castle. "There is another entrance to The Under near the Facilitation Point to The River." Ater spoke aloud under the growing din of the battle. "It's about an hour away if we push ourselves—"

"We push. Now," Pullus interrupted. Grabbing his partner's hand, he pulled Ater to his feet.

Ater looked over his shoulder and saw the ripples in the underbrush already moving toward them. Without another word, the dark elves began to run as the sounds of battle echoed through the night.

The battle for Arcadia had begun.

FERRA had taken three times longer than she needed to pack her gear.

Her mother's possessions had, as was custom, been burnt with her body, so the only things she had to pack were her own. The small heap, a meager amount when compared to the belongings of most Frigus women Ferra's age, had fit easily into her backpack. She sat and stared at her pack for several minutes, trying to ignore the fact that her karmak looked the same as before she had started packing. She heard her roof roll back and Ishia's face poked in. "They said you were leaving."

She sighed and looked back to her pack. "*They* seem to know a lot."

Since she didn't scream at him to leave as she normally did, the teenager took her silence as an invitation and climbed down her ladder. "Why would you leave?" he asked, his voice full of concern; none of their kind ever stepped foot out of the Articus.

"Why would I stay?" she asked, hating the self-pity in her voice though she could do nothing to quell it.

He stood next to her, staring at the pack as well, even though he didn't know why. "I would marry you," he said after a few minutes of silence. She looked over to him, trying to keep the amusement off of her face. "I know," he said, sensing her mirth at his declaration. "I mean, I've heard about your problem." She raised one eyebrow, and he immediately began to backpedal. "Not that I think it's a problem. I mean not a serious problem, at least not to me," he finished. "It is to Logos, not me."

"You think not having a man is my problem?" she asked casually. His eyes grew wide in shock and she laughed it off. "Relax. I am not going to hit you," she assured him. She had indeed punched the last male who had broached the subject with her, so hard his nose whistled when he breathed. "I am asking, if I were to marry you, do you think that would erase my onus? Would I suddenly be welcome among the rest of the tribe?" He looked away, ashamed. She realized he hadn't been aware that she knew what others spoke about her when she was out of earshot. "Do you think it would make Logos love me more?"

The youth's chagrin made her feel better somehow, as if his displeasure proved that not all her people were as petty and hateful as she had been shown of late. The Elders may have been intolerant fools, but there was still hope left for the younger generation. "If I thought it would make a difference," she said, nudging his shoulder, "I would marry you in a second." He looked up with a huge smile. Ferra found it infectious and smiled faintly in turn. “If I were so inclined, I suppose you would not be the worst mate I could think of.” He looked as if he were going to cry, and she knew, out of her entire tribe, she was going to miss him.

“I’ll miss you,” he blurted out quickly.

She held her arms out. “And I suppose I will miss you too.” He grasped her tightly as he tried not to cry into her furs. “You know, once I’m gone you can’t be this emotional,” she cautioned him. He nodded silently, still hugging her. “I mean it. The other boys will tease you mercilessly if they know you’re like this.” He nodded again. She looked down and asked sharply. “Ishia. Are you feeling my breast with your cheek?” He nodded one more time.

She pushed him away as he laughed out loud. “I’m sorry! I wanted to say good-bye to all of you.”

She shook her head as she grabbed her pack off the bed. “I take it all back, I will not miss you.”

He grinned like a loon. “I bet you will.”

She gave him a stern look. “You’d lose that bet.” But they both knew she didn’t mean it.

“Please come back,” he asked earnestly.

She said nothing, knowing if she said she would return, she would be lying. He dropped his stare, understanding her silence. “I’ll walk you to the Elders’ hut,” he offered.

“You shouldn’t,” she said, stopping him. “They are angry enough at me; you don’t want any of their ire.”

“I’m not scared,” he said, adopting the bravest tone he could muster.

She smiled and ruffled his hair. “Keep working on that. You almost sounded like a man.” He cursed under his breath as she climbed out of her karmak and out of her old life.

ABOUT twenty minutes later, Ferra walked back in.

Those twenty minutes had easily been the longest of my life. The five old men spent the time trying to glare at me without making Ruber any angrier than he already was. I, for the most part, ignored them and studied Hawk's sword more closely. When Ferra was holding it, I had easily heard the hum of its energy. In my hands, it had gone silent, but the hilt felt warmer to me. All I could think of was a pocket warmer might have been built into it. Yeah—of course. Even as *I* thought it, the idea sounded stupid.

While Ruber and I waited and the old men glared and muttered and waited, Ruber's earlier words finally penetrated my brain.

"Why is that a good sign?" I asked, looking up at Ruber.

Ruber turned and orientated on me. "Excuse me?"

"You said it was a good sign the sword protected me before. Why is that a good sign?"

"Ah," Ruber replied. Before he said any more, he shifted slightly and flared a bit brighter. I assumed he had seen someone move and had turned his attention back to the magical council of grumpy old men, three of whom sat back down as quickly as they had stood. "The sword is bonded to Hawk's soul; if he were dead, the sword would be effectively dead as well. The fact that it defended you means that, wherever Hawk is, he is at least alive."

The thought that Hawk might have been dead had never actually entered my conscious mind. Not for a second had I even considered the possibility out loud, but from the way the stress and tension lifted off my shoulders, it was obvious some part of me had been thinking the worst. I wiped the moisture from my eyes as I took a second to compose myself before talking again. "So he's okay?" I was finally able to ask.

"His condition I cannot attest to. The sword will continue to function as long as he draws breath, but his actual physical and mental state cannot be determined by the sword alone. For example, he could be in a coma or even brain-dead, but if his heart were still beating…."

"Please stop," I said as I felt myself close to throwing up.

Ruber's voice changed as he realized the effect his words had had on me. In a softer voice he said, "My apologies; that was insensitive."

I sighed as I stood up. "It's okay. He's fine; I know it."

"And how do you know that?" Ruber had to ask.

Before I could answer, our blue warrior walked in. In a lower voice I said to him, "Because he has to be." And I meant it. Hawk had to be okay. There wasn't room in my universe for anything else to happen.

She looked at me, and I could tell she was in no better mood than I was. "You ready?" she asked.

I had to laugh a bit at that. "You're asking me?"

She seemed to get my idea and added a barely audible, "Good point." Turning to the Elders, she stood up straight and said in a stern voice, "Get it over with."

I didn't know what she meant, but the old men sure did. Not even a second passed before the main ugly old man proclaimed, "Ferra, Daughter of Jennia, warrior of the Cold. You are hereby banished from the Frigus for the rest of your life. If you dare to darken our land again—"

I had to give her credit. If she was upset, she didn't show it.

"Right. I have the idea," she said, not giving them time to finish. I saw the pain she was hiding behind her dismissive words. "You ready?"

I nodded. She began to turn toward the door, but I needed to do one thing before we left. I walked to the table and saw the old men's eyes widen with caution. In a voice that sounded eerily like Hawk's, I said, "I am the prince's consort. I will deliver word of your welcome and assistance directly to the ear of Titania and Oberon." I saw their pallor turn from a sea blue to a sky blue, which I took as the Frigus equivalent of paling. "And I am sure the lords of Arcadia will be overwhelmed with your generosity." I saw the oldest one take a halting gulp and knew my threat had been understood. "Count on it, gentlemen."

Then I turned back to Ferra. "Now we can go."

As I walked by her and out the door, I heard her say under her breath, "Thank you for that."

I nodded, knowing I hadn't done it just for her sake.

FLANKED by two enormous parandruses, Puck strode into The Under.

Lumbering on two cloven hoofs, the parandruses were covered in long, dark fur resembling a yak's coat. Each sported a rack of antlers sprouting out from the mop of graying hair that covered its head. Each watched the world from a pair of barely visible, glowing red eyes that seemed to take in the entire marketplace all at once. Wisps of steam issued from their huge nostrils as they shadowed Puck like two trained attack dogs.

Which wasn't too far from the truth.

People in the marketplace fled from the bizarre trio. Most knew who Puck was, and everyone knew Puck's appearance anywhere meant trouble. From the maze of side tunnels that led away from the center of the Dark, more and more curious people began to gather as the ones in the courtyard tried to push past them. No one wanted to get too close to Oberon's emissary, but everyone wanted to hear what he was about to say. Puck waited another couple of minutes, knowing that word spread through the warrens faster than most surface people would imagine. After five minutes, he cleared his throat and began to speak.

"Two dark elves brought a boy down here earlier today." He waited for the words to echo throughout the chamber and be relayed by voices through the tunnels before continuing. "Someone knows where they took him. Tell me now and I will leave."

No one spoke up; no one moved. The sounds of people breathing were faint and stopped when he looked around, his glare baleful.

"They are traitors. Tell me and spare what will happen to you if you don't speak." His voice grew louder, and he saw suspicious looks instead of compliance from the inhabitants of the Dark.

"This is your last chance," he offered, knowing no one was going to talk.

Not a word was spoken.

"I tried," he said to himself and shook his head. He glanced at the parandrus on his right and ordered, "Go," before he looked at the beast on his left and gave the same command.

In a flash they both sprang forward, morphing as they hit the ground. Their forms changed to four-legged feline shapes while their heads shifted into what looked like demonic canines. Their hooves turned into prehensile paws with razor-sharp talons on the ends, which they began to use on the various people who had stayed in the market. Screams sliced the air as the two creatures began to cut a swath of rage-fueled murderous destruction through The Under. Puck shook his head again as he walked to an abandoned pushcart and picked through the food, looking for something decent to eat while he waited.

FERRA took point and Kane and Ruber trailed a few steps behind.

The ruby was able to extend a field of warmth around the human, which was good because the inhospitable nature of the Articus would have killed him within minutes. Kane decided not to say anything more to Ferra, first because she didn't seem like she was in a conversational mood and second because he was breathing hard just trying to keep up.

"So… everyone… just… walks… everywhere?" Kane managed to ask between heaving breaths.

"Some use horses," Ruber replied. He remained completely unaffected by the cold and the pace. "But this far north, they are completely impracticable."

"So… just… walking?" Kane asked again.

"I'm afraid so," the ruby confirmed.

"Awesome," Kane grumbled as he forced himself not to ask Ferra to slow down.

They trekked through the cold for an hour. Inside his cocoon of Ruber-warmth, Kane was sweating. He wondered how the blue girl could maintain her pace and not want to ditch her furs. He began to take his jacket off when Ruber warned him not to. “The cold with your dampness will only invite pneumonia if you were to lose my protection for some reason,” he warned.

“I’m hot!” Kane complained. He knew, the second he said the words, that he sounded like a wimp. “How far until we get out of the Articus?” he finally asked their guide.

“With good weather and the wind at our back,” she said over her shoulder, “a month and a half before we reach the southern lands.”

Kane froze in his tracks.

Ferra took another three steps before she realized the human had stopped following her. She turned back to him. “What?”

“A month? A month at the pace you’re going?” Kane asked.

She shrugged. “I’m starting slow for your sake,” she clarified, planting her spear into the snow. “I assumed you’d get your legs under you sooner or later.”

“A month!” Kane practically screamed. “Are you kidding me?”

Instead of being offended or angered, the warrior looked slightly amused. “Yes, because my people are well known for their sense of humor. How long did you think it was going to take?”

“I don’t know, but not a freaking month,” Kane raged. “My boyf…. Hawk is being tortured right now,” he explained. “We don’t have time for—”

“I cannot control the flow of time nor how far away we are from Arcadia,” Ferra said, obviously annoyed at the boy. “The longer we stay here not moving, the longer our journey will take.”

“He’s in danger!” Kane raged.

Ferra opened her mouth to protest when Ruber floated between them and interjected. “Perhaps we have traveled enough,” he stated diplomatically. “It’s growing dark.”

Kane and Ferra glared at each for a few seconds before she turned away and announced over her shoulder, “We should start a fire.”

“I can keep the boy warm,” Ruber informed her.

“It isn’t for warmth,” she said, not looking back. “The flames keep most beasts away.”

Kane looked at Ruber. “I didn’t like the way she said *most*.”

Ruber found himself silently agreeing.

THE sisters paused as the first screams reached their cave.

Waves of fear and panic radiated throughout The Under in a way the nyxies had never felt before. To them, the emotions were like the wafting scent of a well-cooked steak coming out of nowhere. Although intent on Hawk, all three paused accordingly.

“Trouble,” the youngest thought to her siblings. Her words were tainted with her feelings of concern and anxiety, which was the nyxie equivalent of screaming “Danger!”

“Not directed toward us,” the oldest thought back, her calmness the taste of the air after a heavy rain. “But it is coming nearer and growing.”

The smell had gone from the intoxicating aroma of a barbecue to the stifling smell of a fire burning out of control. “Attack?” the middle sister thought, her confusion and apprehension a tangy cinnamon with just a hint of heat.

Then came the mind-numbingly loud sounds of a being’s last thought before it died horribly. One was followed by two more and then five. All three sisters gasped when the emotional explosions detonated around them as more and more people were slain. Not one of the trio said a word out loud; they didn’t need to.

Every century or so, nyxies fell into a coma-like sleep that lasted anywhere from a year to several decades. When they emerged, they were famished and weak, requiring time to feed themselves before being able to move freely from their nest. The three had only been awake and aware for less than a decade and were still feeding themselves back to health. The prince had provided some sustenance, but nowhere near enough.

The terror and death grew nearer.

The oldest sent her plan and waited for her sisters to absorb it into their psyches. The middle one nodded first, already coming to the same conclusion herself. The youngest, though, seemed confused. Looking down at the unconscious prince and then up at her sisters, she thought, "But we promised."

The oldest mentally slapped her, and the youngest shied away in pain. "Promises with *them* are binding as long as they are useful," the eldest thought sternly. She reached for a blade on the table. "We are beholden to nothing save our own survival." The youngest mentally shielded her mind, cringing and protecting her buffeted psyche from any more attacks. Impatiently, her eldest sister snapped, "Do you wish to die?"

She did not.

"Then we gorge ourselves now," she thought, raising the knife over Hawk's healed chest. "Mother take his soul."

Her hands flew downward, the knife plunging into the fairy's chest with a wet thud.

WITHIN an hour, Ferra had gathered and set up a small collection of wood and twigs along with some dry grass. She used the tip of her spear to break up the hard ground that made up most of the Articus and created a small hole to hold the kindling. Ruber ignited it with his magic, which seemed to impress her greatly, all the more because it saved her own supplies. After that she wandered off across the plains, saying she was going to find us a meal.

"She's not talking like a McDonald's, right?" I asked Ruber.

"Hardly," he answered, clearly uninterested in explaining Frigan food gathering processes any more than he had to.

I picked at the ground with the tip of Hawk's sword. I didn't know proper magic sword etiquette, but I was pretty sure that using a magic anything to dig in the dirt was bad. I just didn't care anymore. I was too worried about Hawk, and sitting there doing nothing was just making it worse. I just wanted to get there *now* but knew that was impossible—even in a magical world. The longer we sat, the harder I dug at the ground, the physical action helping disperse my growing anger.

"If I may interrupt your… gardening," Ruber asked after about thirty minutes, "I have a few questions."

"Shoot," I snapped, not stopping.

"How exactly did I come to be buried in the ground back at the Frigus camp?"

Though his voice still had the crisp British tones I was used to, I could tell the question was important to him by his inflection. I knew what sarcastic Ruber and apathetic Ruber sounded like, and this wasn't either. "Um, they said you were… not moving. So I buried you so you could regenerate in the dirt."

He paused for a few seconds before asking, "Excuse me?"

I stopped my picking and looked up at him. "Well, I assumed because you were a gem elemental that if you were covered in dirt you could… um… you know, get better?" He said nothing. "You know, like Wolverine?" I swear I could imagine the look of disbelief on his face even though, as a gem, he didn't really have a face. "It sounded good at the time," I added quietly.

"You thought that I had the ability to mend myself by simply being covered in dirt?" Though he asked it like a question, I could tell he was just repeating what I had said in exasperation, trying to get the idea through his mind.

"It worked," I said, shrugging.

Before he could respond, Ferra came back and tossed the carcass of a dead wolf to the ground. "I assume you know how to clean and dress that?" she asked.

I looked at the corpse and back to her. "Dress as in clothes?"

She sighed and pulled out a knife. Kneeling next to me and without another word, she began to skin the wolf.

I watched her as long as I could. I had to admit the longer she spent on her task, the more squeamish I became. I looked off as the sun set on the horizon and tried to think of something to say that didn't involve skinning animals or the cold around us. "So… thanks again for coming with us." She made half a grunt as she began to peel the skin off. "I mean, I'm sure it was hard for you to leave your home and all that." I looked back and instantly regretted it, because I couldn't help but see the wolf's carcass.

"It wasn't a hard choice," she said, focusing on her task.

"Still, your family and friends—"

"It is done," she interrupted, looking up at me. "Let's not speak of it anymore."

I closed my mouth and stopped talking.

She efficiently turned the wolf from a dead puppy to meat in less than twenty minutes. As soon as I started to smell the meat cooking, all my vegetarian guilt dissolved in the saliva that filled my watering mouth. We ate in silence as the last light of the day faded away and the night sky filled with stars. I had never seen anything like it on Earth. That thought threw me for a loop. I wasn't on Earth. I was actually on another planet, no, another realm. In a whole other reality, chasing after my not-boyfriend and toting his magic sword so I could return it to him.

I didn't use to have problems like this.

My dad would have loved this. He would have been searching the stars, trying to come up with constellations, probably driving Ferra crazy with his questions. Just thinking about him made me feel even worse. I forced all my depression away as she stood up and started talking.

"I will take first watch. I assume the gem doesn't need to sleep?" Ferra asked when we were done with our meal.

"You assume correctly," Ruber answered her.

"Excellent," she said, moving away from the fire and into the shadows.

"Okay, then," I muttered under my breath. Obviously, Ferra wasn't the chatty type, and trying to make her talk was just going to piss her off even more. I took Hawk's pack and put it down on the ground, wishing I had some kind of blanket or even a jacket to use as a cover.

Something moved inside the pack.

I jumped to my feet, biting my bottom lip rather than screaming like a girl. All I could envision involved snakes or badgers burrowed up inside the pack, waiting to crawl through my hair and bite me in my sleep. "Problems?" Ruber asked, obviously not fazed by my panic.

"There's something in there!" I cried out, pulling Hawk's sword out of my belt with two hands as I did so.

Ruber floated toward the pack, increasing his glow to illuminate the ground. The pack wasn't moving anymore, but something poked out of the top. I pointed at it, and Ruber patiently nudged the pack open. Whatever the something was fell out, dragging more behind it, and I jumped back away. "I believe it is already dead."

I got closer and saw the sleeve of Hawk's jacket.

I hadn't seen it since he'd worn it in school; it must have been stored in the pack. I pulled it out and slipped it on. It was a few sizes too large and smelled like him, which just made me feel even more alone. I wrapped the jacket around me and lay down again. Before I made the pack into a pillow, I looked at it and asked, "You got a pillow in there?"

The pack refused to move.

"Fine," I said, laying my head on it. It wasn't exactly the best, but the pack was the only pillow I had and better than none.

Ruber floated down and, as my eyes adjusted, I could just make out Ferra's back in the darkness. In a whisper I asked, "Why is she so angry?"

His tone subdued, Ruber began to explain. "The people of the Articus are notoriously hard. I believe that the source of her anger is more probably cultural."

"Huh?" I asked confused.

"The Frigus are considered Zero Sum societies." Ruber said Zero Sum like the phrase was supposed to mean something, but I just shook my head. I swear I could hear him sigh, which was a cheap shot since he didn't even breathe. "Their entire culture is based on the fact they have so few resources that every person must contribute in some way. Women are generally valued for childbearing and rearing as well as tending the camp. The fact she is in the warrior caste is proof that she has no interest in having children and is, therefore, not contributing to their society."

That sounded like such bullshit to me. "But she's a badass warrior!" I complained.

"In their culture, she is considered a substandard one, which means her placement was, at best, one made out of pity." Ruber sounded so clinical, like the narrator of a documentary, and I didn't know anymore if he was voicing his own opinions or being an encyclopedia. I was already worried about Hawk, tired after hours of walking miles across the ice and, suddenly homesick, hearing that someone as cool as Ferra would be considered less than anyone else just pissed me off.

"Well, her culture is shit," I said angrily. "If you ask me, the useless ones were the five old geezers messing around in that sweat lodge. What the hell do they—"

The feeling of molten lava being poured into my chest exploded inside me. I clenched at my heart as I screamed out in agony. I saw Ferra running at me as Ruber called out my name, but they both sounded so far away. My brain started to shut out the overwhelming pain that was coursing through me.

I felt the world slipping away from me as I struggled to draw another breath.

CHAPTER SIX

"Beyond the plains, below the mountains,
before the swamps, and just north of the border
runs a River. A River that cuts a nation in two
while it binds the world together. It has been said, and
found to be mostly true, sooner or later all things that are lost
are usually found in The River."
Ballad of The River, Harry Harris

ATER and Pullus ran for their lives.

Although they had neither seen nor heard their pursuers since they'd entered the woods, they both knew the Woolpit Children were still after them. The Children could move silently through the thickest underbrush, making their way as easily as sharks cut through water. Most of the Woolpit Children's prey didn't know they were being hunted until the creatures were almost literally on top of them. Luckily, the dark elves were anything but most people.

Though not bonded with the woods like surface elves, Ater and Pullus had learned to navigate the Boundary Forest surrounding the Dark as if born to it. They ran flat-out, jumping fallen trees and snaking their way through the dense undergrowth at the same pace that other people might run through an open field. Not a word passed between them, but they were in constant communication the entire time through their hands.

Their target was the Facilitation Point an hour's run west of the Dark's main entrance. The point bridged the distance between Arcadia and the world known as The River. It was said that the world was divided by a huge river that was navigated by devices powered with steam magic. Arcadia had opened formal negotiations with the nation known as Americana, a sprawling land that seemed as wild as it was strange. Neither elf had ever traveled to The River, but they had heard the tales that had come from the other side. Its magic seemed to rest in riveted machines that were nothing like the gnome creations that populated the Dark, and they were generally distrusted by everyone. The ambassador for their land was an older, white-haired man who called himself Sam; he always had a multicolor stovepipe hat with him, though he rarely wore it. Beyond those scant facts, neither Ater nor Pullus had much more knowledge.

Both elves knew that crossing over was a bad idea.

Strict rules existed forbidding unscheduled movement from one world to another, primarily because each realm was unique. The laws of nature shifted from realm to realm. The types and levels of civilizations varied from realm to realm. As far as actual Arts, to Ater's knowledge, none existed in The River beyond the strange inventions they created. For anyone traveling to The River who used gear with enchantments on it, or who used The Arts themselves, there was every possibility that their gear and the enchantments might not function properly. But that paled in comparison to the possible reaction the appearance of two dark elves might spark in such a non-arcane realm. Most of the population had no idea of the other realms, and the sudden arrival of two dark-blue-skinned creatures might cause more trouble than it was worth.

The truth of the matter was that the Woolpit Children were gaining on them.

Ater shot a glance to the side and saw Pullus staring back at him. They came to the same conclusion at the same time. They weren't going to make it to the Facilitation Point before the Children overtook them. It was time to change the plan. There were only two choices open to them and, in reality, one of them was no choice at all.

But Ater was still going to give it a try before surrendering to the other.

He could hear Pullus sigh as he slowed his run and turned to fight. Two blades appeared in Ater's hands when he invoked the trigger word in his mind. He brought them up to throw. He didn't even bother to look at his partner, knowing that, even if he didn't agree with Ater's plan, Pullus would back his play. Both knives shot out in a straight line toward the rustling underbrush; he saw an identical pair follow his own less than a quarter second later. A sound much like four blades sinking into a hollow pumpkin in the distance came to their ears, and they glanced at each other, hoping.

Ater flicked his wrists and concentrated on the trigger word again. Both blades appeared back in his hand as he waited to see the results. Three green-faced Children rushed out of the brush, sap-like liquid flowing from gashes in their foreheads. Gashes that were quickly vanishing. If they had suffered even a minor inconvenience from having blades sunk into their skulls, they didn't show it. Pullus launched his knives again into their necks as Ater flipped over them when they reached him. He could see more sap oozing down their necks this time as they rushed under him. Five steps and they slid to a halt, all three at the same time, and turned as one to face their quarry. Without pause, the two injured by Pullus's weapons reached up and yanked the knives out, the cherubic smiles plastered on their faces never wavering.

The sap hardened as the wounds closed themselves and disappeared.

Ater didn't even look over to his partner, already imagining the "I told you so" expression on Pullus's face. The Green Children charged at them, two at Ater, one at Pullus; their bare feet made no sound at all as they ran over a blanket of dead leaves. Both elves spun in place, their roundhouse kicks slamming into The Children's chests, knocking them onto their backs.

Resisting the urge to follow up on their foes' disadvantage, both elves turned and fled toward The River.

Within seconds, The Children gave chase again.

PUCK had torn apart most of the market to make a throne for himself, made up of broken carts and a few abandoned rugs, while he waited. The destruction felt good as he imagined each broken piece of wood as another member of the royal family. He knew the dark elves had hidden the prince somewhere, and he was willing to bet there was at least one person in the Dark who knew.

Puck finished eating his root and tossed the end over his shoulder.

He could hear the sound of battle in the distance and knew the cornered Dark were fighting back. Sighing, he got up from his makeshift throne and headed off to investigate what the delay was. As he rounded the corner from the marketplace, he could hear the roar of a mighty cat echoing down the twisting tunnels of The Under. He found the two parandruses crouched in confusion as their limited intelligence tried to sort out the creature that was facing them.

Puck had heard rumors of a myrmecoleon being kept deep in the tunnels, but he had never seen it with his own eyes. He had to admit it was impressive. Half lion and half ant, the beast had the six legs and segmented body of its insect counterpart; unlike its smaller ant-only cousins, the creature was the size of a great cat. Its carapace was covered with the soft brown fur of a lion. The fur spread into a mane that surrounded its lion head. The only difference between the myrmecoleon's head and that of an actual lion was the pair of unblinking, multifaceted eyes that seemed to view the entire cavern at once. Neither parandrus had seen anything like it before. Both were unsure how to react since it obviously had no intention of backing down.

One of the families down here must have had the ability to control or at the very least communicate with the damned thing, since it was clearly not sentient.

"Quite a watchdog," Puck said to himself, knowing he was running out of time. If the troops upstairs caught wind that an attack was taking place in the tunnels, they would abandon their charge instantly to come to the defense of their loved ones. If they surrendered the attack, the royal guards would follow them down here and slaughter every single man, woman, and child they could find.

Even Oberon would be able to figure out Puck's involvement.

Puck began to shift his form as he walked forward. Creatures like the myrmecoleon were rarely natural creations. They were the results of either experiments in magical crossbreeding or of arcane dabbling by people only interested in pushing the envelope as far as what could be created using The Arts. No matter how many generations removed such a creature might be from the original, they were still basically two different creatures forced into one body. Therefore, the instinctive behaviors of both the lion and the ant were primed to go into action at any given time. Though Puck had never encountered this particular half-breed before, he knew lions and ants quite well.

Lions were animals ruled by dominance, pack creatures that automatically bowed to the strongest specimen in the pack. Ants were all ruled by one queen in a colony.

Puck became a large female ant. Chemical differences between male and female were actually very slight. The significant difference lay in the pheromone the queen emitted; under the control of that pheromone, the entire colony lived to support its queen. When the chemical hit the myrmecoleon, the change was immediate. The ant part of the brute instantly surrendered its will to Puck and the lion part translated that instinct as subservience.

Both reactions were taken by the parandruses as a signal to strike.

A confused sound escaped the lion's mouth as the two shape-shifters tore the beast apart. Puck waited a minute to make sure it was dead before shifting back to his human form. "Stop wasting time!" he barked loudly, knowing if they became gorged on blood they would lose the desire to hunt. When they refused to stop feeding, he strode forward and slapped them sharply on their hindquarters. "*Now!*"

With a begrudgingly angry growl, the pair of parandruses took off back down the tunnels, the taste of blood working them into a frenzy.

Puck was gratified to hear fresh screams echo back toward him, signs that the killing continued.

FERRA rushed toward the camp fire, her spear held point forward, prepared for battle. "What's wrong?" she called out, not seeing what might have felled the boy.

"I'm not sure," Ruber said carefully as he attempted to ascertain what exactly had just happened. "He was fine, and then he collapsed and screamed in pain."

Ferra scanned the surrounding area, cursing the fire as she stared out in the darkness surrounding them. "So we're talking about The Arts?" she asked, trying to ignore the fact she was talking to a floating gem.

A faint red light moved over Kane's writhing form as Ruber tried to answer that very question. "I don't sense an outside spell...," he thought out loud. "And I don't detect a curse."

"Are we under attack or not?" she growled at him.

"I. Do. Not. Know," he replied, his voice icy.

"Then figure it out," she snapped back. "The boy looks like he's dying."

Ruber decided not to respond and went back to scanning the human.

KANE knew the pain wasn't real. His body, on the other hand, did not.

A disconnect such as he had never experienced before had opened between his mind and body. On one hand, he *knew* no one had decided to use his blade like a shovel, digging its point into his chest like a blindfolded four-year-old playing Operation. On the other hand—

There was no other hand.

As much as he knew that he wasn't being flayed alive, as much as his mind battled to remind himself of that, the agony that wracked his body was real. He knew it wasn't but knowing wasn't enough. Somewhere outside of him, Hawk experienced the true horror; that much Kane knew as well. His rational mind scrabbled for purchase and screamed that what he thought he was suffering was an echo, a part of the horror that had struck down Hawk.

No, that wasn't quite right. The echo originated within him but wasn't a part of him, not completely. Kane would have laughed if he could have at the fierce internal debate his mind waged, but the spasming of his body as the agony worsened crushed any sounds other than moaning and screaming.

The pain was coming from somewhere deep inside him, somewhere he'd only discovered recently. It emanated from the same place that pulsed with warmth every time Hawk smiled at him. Hawk.

Though his instinct was to run as far away as he could from the pain, Kane forced himself to see it and then to concentrate on it. To treat it as an entity, to see its size, and to find a way through it, try to find its true source. Although his eyes were closed both physically and mentally, he flinched when he turned to stare directly at its scalding, pulsing white heat. "Stay. Stay," was all he heard himself mutter. One faltering step and then another, and he needed to stop. Everything *burned*. His entire being shook in reaction to the hurt, but he forced himself past it. *Hawk, I'm coming.* More heat, more torture. He felt like he was going to burst into flames. *No!* Kane let loose a primal scream and dove at the genesis of it all.

The pain vanished, giving way as if it had been no more than a curtain disguised as a brick wall.

Kane felt himself falling into a great void that was every bit if not more terrifying than the pain had been. He couldn't even hear his own voice as he cried out for help. A hand grabbed his and stopped his descent instantly. The sensation of gravity evaporated around him as he felt himself floating.

"You scream like a girl," a voice said from behind him.

Kane turned and saw Hawk standing there, holding his hand.

THE pain, the void, everything simply vanished as I rushed toward him. I felt his arms wrap around me and I hugged him tight. My mouth refused to work, swamped by the thousand questions flooding my brain simultaneously. Instead of feeling frustrated because I didn't know what to say, I felt only relief and happiness when I looked up and saw Hawk smile.

I could see myself in his eyes, see every single second we had spent together, and feel the emotions he had felt looking at me. Even though I was a phantom also, I could feel myself blush at the vastness of his love. There were no doubts, no conditions in his mind at all. He looked at me and saw a rock in the center of his world, a center for him always and everywhere. There were no boundaries to his faith. I was awed by it until I realized it was what had been connecting us the entire time. I looked into his eyes and saw myself reflected back into infinity, like a mirror looking at itself. It was a perfect moment, a moment of just him and me and everything we were laid out between us.

And then it was gone.

I saw Hawk flinch as he grasped his chest. A half second later, I felt a pain rush through my own chest. He opened his mouth to say something but there was no sound. All I got was the blind pain and fear he was feeling as he was yanked away from me. I watched him struggle against whatever had him, and I fought to reach, to hold him and keep the pain away, to no avail. I had nothing to push against. I just floated there and watched him be taken from me.

The pain in my chest flared again and I curled myself against it, knowing it was as much a phantom as I was in that place.

Except this time, something I'd seen plunged into my chest before had been thrust into me again.

It was Hawk's sword.

I grasped the hilt with both hands and screamed when the sword moved in the injury it had carved. All I knew was that I had to pull it out. Every inch was agonizing, but I knew what I was going through couldn't begin to compare to what Hawk was feeling. He was in pain. I needed to get to him. Nothing else mattered. Halfway out, the sword flared with power and I felt myself tumble backward into the dark void. My speed increased immeasurably and I squeezed my eyes shut, but the darker void outside invaded my being until I was just as dark as it.

I slammed into something and blacked out.

TWO guards stood the watch at every Facilitation Point at all times.

Though the assignment was largely ceremonial, they served as an early warning system rather than a martial deterrent. It had been so long since any of the realms had openly moved against another that security had become nothing more than routine. One guard stood on either side of the massive circle of water that floated perfectly above the ground. Mounted on a stone dais, there were three steps leading up to it, the opening of a whirlpool that had no depth in that world, a perfect circle of water that seemed to fall sideways as it spun clockwise. The two men on duty right now no more expected an attack from The River than they expected to sprout wings and start laying eggs.

Which is why Ater and Pullus took them out within seconds.

Both men slumped over and hit the ground as the dark elves sprinted by them. The Children broke from the forest's cover, their camouflage useless given the lack of trees and shrubbery near the Facilitation Point. Pullus, in the lead, launched himself off the top step and leapt toward the circle. His hands grabbed the top of the portal. Half a second behind, Ater replicated the move, except he grabbed his partner's legs instead. They swung forward into the gateway, a bizarre trapeze act.

The Second's hand gripped the edge of the portal as he swung into the water. His feet and lower legs disappeared into The River along with all of Ater, who still hung on to Pullus's calves. Focused on capturing their prey, the Children followed Ater. Pullus heard the roaring of water as The River pulled everything into its path, including the Green Children.

Half a moment and Pullus swung himself back to the Arcadian side of the Point. His muscles strained as he hauled Ater from The

River and back to dry land. The force of the water was diminished since Pullus was still technically on the Arcadian side and Ater was connected to him.

The other elf was drenched. He dropped to the ground, let out a loud gasp, and then struggled to draw breath. Pullus went to his knees, his pants soaked from the brief exposure to the other side. "You all right?" Pullus panted. All Ater could manage was a nod before he went back to breathing.

Even though Ater had been on The River for perhaps fifteen seconds as they were measured in Arcadia, Pullus knew his partner had spent much more actual time trying not to drown. Time moved very differently in The River; because of the way time and space varied between the realms, what was seconds to Pullus was most likely minutes for the other man.

Since The River's Facilitation Point lay physically beneath Arcadia's, a shift in both physical location and gravitational pull occurred whenever a being made the crossing. The traveler went from moving horizontally through the Facilitation Point to falling suddenly when the transition completed. And since The River's medium was largely water, the unwary individual might find himself being swept away in the rushing current rather than being hauled in by the guard on The River's side of the crossover point. Both Elves had known that as long as one of them was still connected to the Arcadian side, The River could not take them. The Children had nothing to brace themselves against and so were swept through to the other side, dragged by the current against their will.

"I hate this plan," Ater said after catching his breath.

Pullus smiled at him as he pulled him to his feet. "Well, between you and me, you needed the bath."

Ater playfully swung at him in response. Pullus caught Ater's hand and pulled his partner close. When he looked up, all he saw was the warmth and love in Ater's eyes. There was no time to delay so they settled for leaning against each other, foreheads touching.

"Ready?" Pullus asked after a second, knowing the Children would undoubtedly cross back over once they had regained their bearings. He wondered idly whether being on The River would affect them since they were elementals of this world. He squeezed Ater's hands and nodded encouragingly.

Ater nodded, trying to ignore the chill the night air wrapped around him.

They took off as one toward The Under.

I BOLTED upright, still fighting off the nightmare, still reaching for Hawk.

I saw Ferra jump as I gasped loudly. Ruber floated away from me, which I assumed was the equivalent of a startled movement for him. I blinked but I could still see Hawk screaming in front of me, like the afterimage from staring too long at the sun. Hesitantly, Ferra asked me, "Are you… better?"

I squinted to focus on her; for a moment I had no idea who she was. I realized Hawk would have looked at her the same way if he had been here. "No," I said, standing quickly, then tottering before finding my balance. "We need to get to Hawk. Now," I added, sliding his jacket on and grabbing the pack.

"How?" Ferra asked, her annoyance pushing past her obvious concern. "I told you the trip is a long one…."

"She is right, Kane," Ruber agreed slowly, sounding a lot like he was trying to talk sense into a crazy person.

Which probably wasn't so far off.

"I saw him," I said. "I mean, I felt him. I can still feel him. We're connected."

"I see," which was Ruber for *I don't believe a word of what you're saying, but I'm too polite to bring it up.* "And that changes things how?"

“It means we’re connected,” I repeated, pulling Hawk’s blade out. “This is connected to both of us… to… I don’t know, but it is!” I struggled to put the concepts in my head into words.

“It is connected to Hawk, I agree,” Ruber said carefully. “But how does that change our location?”

“Because it’s connected to me also,” I blurted out, hoping whatever the blade was supposed to do would somehow make itself known.

“It’s connected to his soul,” Ferra explained. When I looked at her, she nodded at the blade. “The blade, it was forged with a portion of his soul in it.”

When I looked at the sword again, I could tell she was right. It felt like Hawk, that same feeling as when he was close to me. “Exactly. So if it’s connected to his soul, then it can find him.”

“Yes,” Ruber agreed in a tone that said he was either thinking Ferra’s words and my logic over or still trying to appease the crazy guy. “That may be true, but it doesn’t get it to Hawk.”

“No!” I said, shutting him up. “If the blade is connected to him, it can open a portal to him. It’s just a matter of focusing.” As I said the words, I saw the sword begin to glow brighter. “After all, it’s a sword. It can cut us a path.” The brightness increased with each word. It understood. The sword understood!

The sword’s blade turned from silver-blue to gold to a blinding white and began to whine in my hands. I had no idea what I was doing when I pointed the weapon at a spot where the air had begun to shimmer, but I focused every bit of my will on Hawk. Only Hawk.

FERRA sidled closer to Ruber. “The boy knows it is impossible for the weapon to actually pierce the veil, correct?” she asked, referring to reality in the words of her people. “That can’t be done.”

Kane was just a shapeless shadow in the nimbus of light the blade was producing.

"I don't believe the boy does know that," Ruber commented, watching the impossible unfold in front of him.

The sound of The Arts being channeled into the area was deafening. Amid the roar of wind and water circling ever tighter around him, Kane began to move the blade in an easy vertical ellipse. Summoned by the magics of the blade, The Arts aided it in its work and the air wavered visibly. Still relaxed, Kane waited until the sword resisted and then tightened the circle, while The Arts found one note and kept it. Tighter and louder the sound grew, more taut and increasingly focused on one place, one word, the sword. Both Ferra and Ruber backed away as the sound buffeted them. The Frigus covered her ears as the intensity funneled every bit of energy into a pinpoint in time.

Abruptly, Kane snapped the blade directly overhead and brought it crashing down through the light and the noise. The air parted under the assault.

The sound of reality being torn asunder moved through them so they actually heard it from the inside out. In front of them, Kane watched his handiwork, oblivious to everything else. He held the sword easily and with grave familiarity as it became a sword once again, its task done for the moment, while the light that had enfolded him and the sword faded.

Ferra could not believe what she was seeing.

In front of the boy was a hole in the air. She caught a glimpse of green, perhaps. Somewhere else. Green. Not white....

Kane craned his head around and stared at both Ferra and Ruber. "Come on, move!"

Without a thought, he jumped through the hole and was gone.

"That's impossible," she said to Ruber, still not sure what had just happened.

"Yes," he agreed, floating toward the rift. "Yet it is still happening. I suggest moving."

She shook herself out of her stupor and followed the gem into the steadily shrinking hole in the world. Within seconds it had disappeared, leaving the fire to burn alone in the middle of nowhere.

IMAGINE being asleep.

Imagine a slumber so deep that there are no dreams or sensations, just the numb silence of catatonia. Now imagine the slow moments before you wake up. The duality that you are partly awake and yet mostly asleep, on that small patch of beach between the deep waters of dream and the sandy shores of the waking we all walk every time we open our eyes to the day. Imagine as you come to consciousness, before you are fully awake, that you hear someone screaming in pain. The sound comes from very far away but grows stronger the moment you acknowledge it.

Because it is a dream, you fall upward, a diver hurtling from the darkened depths of your subconscious toward the light of your waking mind. The closer you move toward reality, the louder the screaming becomes, and your chest starts to itch. Instinct tells you to scratch, but you realize your limbs no longer belong to you, and you remain totally motionless. The itch starts to burn and the scream turns into sobbing wails as you thrash vainly against your paralysis. The burn begins to sink past your skin and into your very soul as the last veil of the dreaming is peeled away.

It is only then that you realize the screams are yours, and that is when the pain starts.

HAWK wakes in a panic, his throat already sore from screaming.

There is nothing in his world save the raw and exposed pain that was once his chest. He can feel hands crawling at what has to be an open wound as he lies there unable to stop them. There is a sound that reminds him of fresh meat being torn asunder as another wave of pain moves through him. It takes him a few seconds of shrieking before he can identify it as the sounds of his assailants clawing into the exposed hole in the center of his chest as they try to open the wound further. He hears a bone snap and his mind slips back into shock. His body refuses to move no matter how hard he pushes.

This was not how he imagined dying.

His thoughts race toward the image of Kane and, though his world is made up of scarlet waves of agony, he pauses, imagining the other boy's crooked smile.

Another snap of bone and the moment is lost. He begins screaming again.

CHAPTER SEVEN

"The only known battle to take place on Arcadian soil was the attempted coup d'état initiated by the Family Crimson shortly before The Ascension. It is said the Monarch Demain would stop at nothing to stop Titania from making Faerth the center of the realms."

A Brief History of Arcadia

Raatnaraj Ruber Scientia

THE first burrower broke the surface of the courtyard before dawn.

The garrison manning the walls didn't even notice until the swarms of goblins screaming their garbled battle cries issued from the hole. The guards had been so intent on the chaotic waves of creatures outside the crystal wall that the castle had been breached before they knew it. Though caught off guard and heavily outnumbered, the guards ignored the walls and began shooting into the crowd, each shot killing a goblin instantly. But there were only so many arrows and far more goblins.

Within ten minutes, despite heavy losses, the rebellion claimed the courtyard.

A single flare launched from the helm of the lead burrower signaled "Go" for the next phase of the assault. As the goblins feasted on their fresh kills, the crow spirits that had been blocking the flow of magic into the capital reversed their curse, amplifying the ley lines' power instead of nullifying it. Outside the walls, the two naga witches who had been waiting began to chant, their always-formidable power made impossibly strong by the extra magic. Their forked tongues spat out curse after curse as they began to hurl bolts of energy at the wall.

Nine minutes into the attack, the first crack appeared in the magical crystal. A roar went up from the mass of attackers as it began to fracture.

With the enchantment broken, the walls shattered underneath the weight of the rushing mob. Hundreds were trampled underfoot as the makeshift army surged forward, but no one paused. Of course, none of the mob knew they were being affected by the half dozen Phobias that lurked invisibly behind the front and projected waves of terror at the group randomly. All the creatures knew was that their very lives depended on breaching the walls of the castle proper.

Fourteen minutes into the attack, the walls disintegrated.

And the mob froze where it stood. Waiting.

No one dared move toward the castle itself. So far the attack had gone off like clockwork, but breaching the wall was as far as any of them had been told to go. They waited anxiously for Trias's commands to be passed forward from the command tent. In the meantime, the Alp-luachra began to feast on the few bones left by the goblins after they had gorged themselves on the guards they'd killed. The Alp's newt-like bodies clung to the bloody limbs as they drank greedily.

Within minutes Trias's second, the brownie, appeared in a cloud of dust. Everyone paused to hear his words.

The miniscule creature looked around at all the impatient faces and took a deep breath before screaming at the top of his lungs, "*Ogres*!" Then he was gone.

The ground beneath them crumbled when six massive ogres breached the tunnels and exploded out of the holes. Bodies fled in all directions as the enraged beasts peered at the menagerie of beings the same way a well-fed lord looks at a buffet. A *freyburg* moved too late and its howls echoed throughout the courtyard as an ogre tore a bite out of the black dog's side. A *haetae* made the mistake of roaring in anger at another ogre and ended up having the side of its face caved in for its trouble. The half lion, half dog whimpered as the ogres left its twitching body in the courtyard while they looked around. Everyone else wisely began to flee when the deformed giants moved toward them.

Three naked women with hair almost down to their ankles made their way past the crowd and fearlessly confronted the ogres. Their smiles were identical and their almond-shaped, unblinking eyes had no pupils. They seemed almost more doll than human as they looked up at the berserk ogres.

As one, they began to sing.

The ogres stopped as if slapped, the expression of rage and fury melting into bemused smiles that made them look intoxicated. The three sang in a language no one alive could decipher, but their intent was clear to the enthralled ogres. The six beasts turned toward the castle and in a military shuffle walked to the doors, their massive hands clenching and unclenching in anticipation of more destruction. They got up four of the seven steps to the castle unopposed.

When they reached the fifth step, the doors burst open and Oberon and his guards charged the ogres.

The battle for the capital had finally begun.

RUBER had never seen anything like it.

The boy, the human boy, the human boy with no Arts training whatsoever, had used a sword to cut a hole in reality. The ways in which this was patently impossible were too numerous to mention. Least of all was the fact that neither the sword nor the boy had any means of bypassing The Nowhere as the portal obviously had. Senders required years and years of study and practice to slice open passages through the air like the one Kane just created; to see that ability imbued into a lifeless artifact was unheard of. Magic like that was barely controlled by mages who had studied for centuries. For a human boy and a sword to do it was flat-out impossible.

The sword, though bonded with Hawk and carrying part of his soul, was not sentient. Since the sword did not have the mind to transport them instantly from the Articus to The Under and neither he nor Ferra knew what Kane intended, only Kane was left as the impetus.

Which was, still, utterly impossible.

Yet, as Ruber floated out the other side of the portal, he instantly knew he was indeed in The Under. Ferra walked though seconds after, and the look of complete distrust on her face was telling. Most of her people would have run in terror from such a display of The Arts. Fortunately, Ferra was not most of her people. She might have wanted to have some words with Kane about her journey; however, they had teleported into the middle of a slaughter.

Ruber identified the beasts as a pair of parandruses wading through the running crowds of people. Indiscriminately severing limbs and heads as they went, they took time every now and then to eat a particularly choice piece of meat before cutting their way through the masses again. Kane, clearly exhausted after his feat, rested a hand against the cave wall for support.

Ferra had no such pause.

She let loose a scream so intense that the parandruses froze in place, shook their heads to clear the ringing in their ears and, when she screamed her battle cry again, spun around in shock to face the source of the noise. The closest received the point of her spear lodged in its left eye. The instant the tip touched the creature's face, ice began to form around the wound, freezing the burst eyeball and blood, covering the whole socket within a second. As it reared back from the pain, Ferra dug her feet in and pulled the spear free. The entire left half of the parandrus's face shattered like broken glass. The second creature, still not sure what had just happened to its mate, rushed the blue-skinned stranger with all its might. Ferra brought her spear up and braced for the impact.

"Protect."

Neither Ferra nor the beast looked toward Ruber's voice, but they did react to the shield that appeared between them. Unable to stop its momentum, the parandrus slammed into the energy form, the crash of the collision accented by the sound of breaking bones. Ferra, not sure if she had just been saved or captured, touched the tip of her spear to Ruber's shield; a small lattice of ice formed on its surface and then quickly melted away.

"Be ready," Ruber said to her. "I am dropping the shield."

She nodded and glared at the parandrus, whose broken bones were slowly mending as it got to its cloven hooves. "I'm ready."

Ruber dropped the shield.

If she had been human, her speed would have been surprising. With one thrust she plunged the spear into the beast's chest, then, using the weapon as a pole, vaulted over it and attacked its wounded mate. The parandrus managed one wheezing sound before the interior of its chest froze solid. By the time Ferra landed on the other side of it, the beast was already dead, its heart now encased in ice along with its lungs and upper intestines. The second one snarled at her out of half a face, although the exposed bones had already knitted back and a fine film of muscle was just trying to form over it. Something moved in the empty eye socket but Ferra paid it no mind.

"In the name of Logos, I claim this kill!" she screamed, slamming the spearhead down on the center of the creature's skull. Ruber extended a shield over Kane, who was still leaning heavily against the tunnel wall, to protect him from the ice shards that exploded from the impact. The parandrus's body seemed to shift slightly, as if it wasn't quite aware it was already dead. Its fur went as white as an Articus bear for a moment before darkening to a jet black.

They both died within seconds of each other.

Ferra stood there, her breath fogging in the air as she battled to calm her body from the combat rush she was still experiencing. Ruber watched as the two parandruses melted into deflated corpses that were, in reality, nothing more than withered skins.

"Impressive," he said quietly, not sure if he should interrupt her moment of silence.

She glanced at the floating rock and truly smiled for the first time since they had met her. "It's warm." She beamed.

He was about to answer when Kane clutched at his chest and screamed out in pain. Ruber could swear he heard another cry echo somewhere deeper in the catacombs.

"*Hawk!*" the human cried, running through Ruber's barrier as if it were nothing more than light.

"How did he do that?" Ferra asked, knowing how solid the barrier was from personal experience.

Ruber began to follow Kane down the darkened tunnel. "I have no idea," he called back to her as she followed him. He was beginning to loathe saying those four words.

I FELT like I was going to die.

I don't mean that in an "Oh my God, the wrong David won *American Idol*" kind of way. I mean, honestly, who picks Collective Soul over John Lennon anyway?

I mean it in a "My chest feels like someone is making a jack-o'-lantern out of it, and I have a bad feeling they are about to put the candle in and light it" way. Rationally, which was a word I wouldn't have gone within five miles of before the last few days, I knew the pain wasn't mine. I knew it was phantom pain, not part of my body but still very real to my mind.

The pain was Hawk's. Knowing that didn't make anything better at all.

I have no idea how the sword made the portal, but it felt like whatever it used had come from me, a big part of me. I leaned against the tunnel wall trying to catch my breath and out of nowhere, I remembered the day we had to run that mile for the First Lady's physical fitness thing in school. Which was a crock because I didn't see *her* out there running with us. Jewel and I had run like there was a pack of rabid Taylor Swift fans after us. Our gym teacher had warned us that whoever came in last was going to end up with mandatory laps for the next three weeks as a reward.

That day, my lungs had felt like they were on fire and my legs got some kind of muscle Alzheimer's because they just flat-out forgot how to walk, run, or even stand upright. I had felt like a teenage-size infant, ready to drop dead at any moment. At that time, I really thought that was the worst I was ever going to physically feel.

Boy, did I judge that one wrong.

Every part of me wanted to rush to Hawk—every part but my body, that is. The exhaustion I felt rose from deep inside me, flowing relentlessly outward and permeating every cell of my body. I wasn't sweating or panting for breath; I felt drained. I knew that if I had to take just one step, I'd fall because my muscles couldn't help me. If I had to describe it, I would say my soul was exhausted and it needed a nap in a big, bad way.

Ferra screamed something off to my left, and I saw Ruber's shield out of the corner of my eye, but what they were doing meant nothing to me. You know that feeling, when you're really lightheaded and you have an out-of-body sensation? Like everything is happening really far away and not to you, and you still know it is but can't do anything about it?

Well then, you pretty much know where I was for those seconds/hours.

I might have passed out if a new stab of pain hadn't shot through me/Hawk, waking me up from my stupor something quick. The same way you can feel cold water filtering through you on a hot day. I could almost see the adrenaline that sparked through me. This time I could feel him and knew he was nearby. I have no idea why, but I thought his name as hard as I knew how. It felt like one of those lame radar things you see in submarine movies. Something hit me from outside and pinged me, and I pinged him back.

God, that sounds so lame.

The certainty that I was close to him slammed everything back into focus. I ran down the hallway… um, tunnel… the tunnel hallway… whatever. I ran down the long, dark, rock tunnel hallway toward him. I didn't look back to see if Ruber was following; I didn't scream over my shoulder where I was going. Hawk was in trouble and he needed me.

That was the only thing that mattered.

If I had stopped to think for even a second, I would have ended up lost. Luckily for me, when it comes to Hawk, thinking is not my strong suit. Left, left, right, past the wall covered with tacky vines that looked like the kind of thing a druid hangs up when he goes away to college and wants some privacy from his roommate. The image that I must look like a bloodhound passed through my mind, but I had every bloodhound there ever was beat, hands down. I was half a person looking for my other half.

My better half, if I had to tell the honest truth.

That thought almost stopped me cold. My better half? Where did that thought come from? He was everything you would want in a Disney prince. Handsome, good hair, blinding white smile, and a magic sword. He was fearless, honorable, and way, way out of his depth when it came to solving his problems, but why did I think that made him better than me? Another, much weaker scream brought me back to the moment. I'd think later. I ducked beneath a low ceiling that would definitely have stopped me very cold if I'd hit it and found the passage in the back of it that led to a hidden chamber.

The sword raised, I burst into the room and saw the three hot chicks swaying over my man. My man? Where was this coming from?

They looked like a pack of cheerleader vampires the way they hovered over his open chest, their faces smeared with his blood as he moaned in pain. You'd think the small details would be lost on me in such a moment, but it was the opposite. I could see the way his fingertips were bloody from trying to claw at the stone altar he sprawled on, meaning he had been there suffering for a while. He was lying in a pool of blood that had turned dark and cooled by now, his hair was matted with it and it made me sick. And his screams; I will never forget his screams.

I think I should also add, I noticed all this as I leapt at the nasty skanks, Hawk's sword ready.

My first swing sliced the neck of the skank opposite me, the sword hitting under her chin and angling upward and back.

Remember, Hawk, when swinging at a creature's head, the best tactic is to come in at an angle, lifting upward. Though you may be physically stronger than most of the enemies you meet, even the frailest creatures' necks and spinal columns can reduce a killing blow into the equivalent of chopping wood. That will slow you down and distract you, leaving you open to attack. If you swing upward, you have a better chance of separating the vertebra, effectively paralyzing or killing the creature.

I tried to ignore the memories that came with my newfound fighting skills, but my/Hawk's muscle memory apparently needed the visual flashback to work. The sword had lodged itself in the bitch's neck, almost all the way through. I knew I needed a few seconds to pull it free from her corpse and knew just as clearly that her two sisters were not going to give me those seconds.

The key to swordplay is not *strength. Any idiot can pick up a blade and kill someone; it takes speed and agility to do it effectively. Movement! You must always stay moving if you want to have any chance of winning a sword fight. Only an idiot stands and swings.*

I pivoted to my left, using a Wonder Woman-like spin to haul the sword clear of the first woman's neck. Keeping my momentum, I lifted the sword and chopped it down, slicing a good portion of the second's face off with my strike. She screeched as I cut through one cheek, her mouth, and came out the other side, taking what looked like her tongue along on the edge of the sword. I could feel the memory of Hawk's abilities shake its invisible head at my style as I teed off on her like I was holding a baseball bat instead of a bladed weapon. The ragged scream that garbled from her throat never finished. I kicked her back with one foot as hard as I could. She impacted with one of the braziers of oil that had been supplying light for their hot guy buffet and she went up like she was made out of straw.

No matter how much I wanted to watch Morticia number two run around the cave doing her best Michael Jackson Pepsi commercial impersonation, I could feel the third one moving behind me. I turned to face her but was too late. Her hands grasped the sides of my face as she locked eyes with me.

I heard the word "Pain!" in my head as something passed from her to me in the air.

This time the pain was neither phantom nor disconnected from me; this time the horror was all mine. My body spasmed as every nerve ending I had burst into flames. I felt myself clench into a ball, Hawk's sword falling from my grasp as I hit the ground. Instead of reaching a high point and then retreating before returning like most pain did, this just ratcheted higher and higher, each second more unbearable than the last. I want to say I didn't make some weak-ass whimpering sound, but for all I knew I was pissing myself when she knelt down, her fingers hovering just over my body as she drank in my emotions.

"So much pain, so much delicious pain," her voice echoed in my head. I so wanted to be the action hero and throw something witty back at her as I clenched my teeth and bore the pain in a manly fashion, but I didn't. I just rocked myself, wishing whatever she was doing would stop.

"You want pain?" Hawk's voice resounded in my head. "Take all you want."

The vampire chick's screams were louder than anything I had ever experienced. Hawk stopped trying to shield me from his pain and let it flow through whatever weird-ass X-Men telepathy we shared. I have no idea what he did, to be honest; one second she was all Big Red from *Bring It On* lording her superiority over me, the next she was scrambling to get away from my mind as Hawk dropped all but the thinnest of shields around me to keep me from his pain while he diverted my pain into the monster. The pain from the torture, the wounds, everything that he'd been feeling was suddenly shoved down her throat. Whatever she was, I could feel her try to disengage her "talons" from my mind to escape, but Hawk pinned her mind in place, forcing her to experience in the span of ten seconds what she and her three sisters had been doing to him for hours.

Suffice it to say, mystical emotion-stripping vultures cannot take it as well as they dish it out.

Her skin began to bubble, and I crawled a few steps back because every time I had seen that in a movie, it meant their head was going to explode like a ripe watermelon. The flaps of skin that covered her eye sockets began to inflate and she clawed at them with fingers that resembled overstuffed sausages of rotting meat. In a matter of seconds, her blonde and silky hair went from looking fit for a shampoo commercial to a dirty mop that hadn't been rinsed in years.

I tried to get to my feet and settled for lurching a few more steps from her.

The worst part was the screams.

If they'd come out of her mouth, putting my hands over my ears might have helped mute the volume. But they ricocheted from her to my mind and back to her and back again, worse and louder every time. Hawk funneled more and more pain into her but—but—

Hawk!

I felt what happened before I really recognized it. Hawk had been protecting me from the worst of the pain, but he was losing strength, and the shield he'd put in place had begun to fail. I figured that out at the same instant the skank's head exploded.

Hawk! was all I could think. He lay sprawled on the stone thing, his chest torn open and his body finally giving up on him. I only noticed the light that was part of him when it died. His voice in my mind faded farther away as I pushed through the heap of floozy leftovers to get to him.

I screamed his name, my mind to his mind, and I swear I heard him say my name back while he struggled to reach me with his nearest hand.

Instead of taking it I reached down, picked up his sword, and plunged it into his chest as hard as I could.

That was when things got weird.

CHAPTER EIGHT

"Life is fleeting. The soul is eternal."
Veritas Speculum

THE ogres went down so fast that the goblin "troops" immediately behind them weren't even aware the behemoths had been defeated until they heard the people around them begin to scream in fear. The fairies had trained literally decades for battles such as these and had been begging for the chance to fight the insurgents for weeks. Oberon and his guards cut a swath of death, mowing down the stunned goblins and leaving their carcasses like so much kindling in the courtyard.

The goblins had been promised fresh kills and an ample quantity of dwarven mead if they participated in the attack. That promise and some basic "Walk forward together and hack anything that's not a goblin—the kills are yours" constituted their training.

The result wasn't so much an attack as a slaughter. The first line of goblins was dispatched with such fierce, accurate swordwork that some kept walking even after their heads had been severed or their arms hacked off. By the time the rear of the goblin line realized the battle plan was not working as intended, it was too late. The guards decimated them as surely as any bird of prey stooping from three thousand feet to snatch an unsuspecting field mouse.

The survivors of the first onslaught attempted to escape. They did not get very far.

In the rebels' camp, Trias waited for one of his scouts to return. The sounds of screaming coming closer and closer meant that Oberon had entered the fray. Two seconds later, a horrified brownie appeared, white as milk, its breath coming so fast it made a whistling sound. "Retreatwemustretreat!" it kept saying over and over again.

"I wish," the elemental said under his breath. Ignoring the panicked scout, he moved the table aside and knelt down; the sound of cracking wood filled the tent until he was on one knee. Slowly he began to wave his hands over the earth in wide circles, his eyes closed as he quietly chanted. At first nothing happened but within a moment, the packed dirt began to vibrate and rise in one spot near Trias's bent knee. Something emerged from the depths below. A silent fall of soil marked the breach in the ground as the top of an iron chest broke the surface. Trias frowned when he realized that every side of the chest had been engraved with sigils and signs. He couldn't decipher them, for they were covered with stubborn soil, but the purpose of the mystical signs was clear. Only the correct person would be able to open the box. Anyone or anything else would die.

When the chest was fully unearthed, Trias sighed. "How did you know it would come to this, Puck?" he asked the air. His twig-like fingers touched the surface of the cold metal and the markings began to glow with blood-red energy.

"Robin Goodfellow," he said, uttering the phrase Puck had told him would disarm the enchantment.

The glow vanished as something inside the chest let out a muffled click. Slowly the lid opened. The matchstick man held his breath as he waited for the contents to be revealed. He had never been privy to what had been placed inside. All he knew was that it should be opened and used only if the rebellion's main attack met disaster. Over the weeks, he had imagined all sorts of demonic items that could have been secreted within the Pandois Chest. Whatever it held, Trias had hoped he would be called on to wield it.

A solitary scroll sat inside, coiled up tight like a snake ready to strike.

"This is our doomsday weapon?" he asked, half disbelieving, half angered as he retrieved the vellum, noticing as he did that the wax which closed it bore a royal seal. He puzzled for a second, not recognizing the mark. Well, sealed or not, Puck had told him to open the contents of the chest. Sliding one finger under the wax, he sliced it in half impatiently. He completely missed the glimmer of power released by his action. Unrolling the scroll, he began to skim over the first few words, never realizing he was already dead.

Four seconds later, the tent exploded in fire.

RUBER and Ferra rounded the corner in time to see Kane pick up Hawk's sword and plunge it toward the prince's chest.

"*Protect!*" Ruber cried, casting his shield farther than he ever had before to extend over Hawk's motionless form across the cavern. The shield might as well as been made of paper, because the sword cut through it without pause.

Ferra heard the gem cry out in pain as it fell out of the air. Truheart's power shot magical feedback through the gem. Ignoring her racial hatred of all things magical, she lunged for him as he plummeted downward. She caught him inches before impact and then stopped dead still when the glow inside him began to flicker wildly, as if someone had set a fire within him. She wasn't sure whether to drop the gem in case he exploded or to try somehow to heal him.

So engrossed was she in Ruber's plight, Ferra never heard Puck skulking up behind her.

Years of training coupled with blind luck resulted in her keeping a whole spine. Instead of a killing blow, all he managed to inflict were three deep wounds across her lower back. Ferra automatically threw herself forward and into a roll at the first sign of trouble. The injuries threw off her concentration and she hit the cave floor, a loud grunt of anger her only acknowledgment of her injuries. Ruber rolled away from her under his own power as she scrambled around to meet her attacker head-on.

Puck's face melted like wax as he shifted from his hobgoblin form into that of a raven-black cave troll. Nine feet tall with skin tougher than hardened leather, he roared a challenge and slammed down at Ferra with his razor-sharp talons.

She felt the ground shake as she rolled away from the blow.

So that's not allowed to hit me again, she thought while she struggled back to her feet. Her back screamed in protest but she pushed past the pain, dodging when the changeling swiped at her again. His blows indicated great power but relatively little skill. The cave troll, true to its kind, lunged at her wildly, swinging twice as she stayed clear of the attack. She carefully watched Puck pull his claws free of the cave's stone floor where his last swinging blow had lodged them. The shape-shifter might have the intelligence of a human being but, in the form of a cave troll, he fought like a troll would. There was no skill, no forethought, just raw power in his swings. While part of her brain wondered how much his race became the creatures they mimicked, the other part of her mind formulated a plan.

She grabbed her spear with both hands and turned to face her aggressor. Halfway through the motion, she cried out in pain. As one of her hands moved to her wounds, she went down on one knee. Puck took the opportunity to rear his right hand back and swing at her with as much force as he could muster.

Before Puck could react, she pushed herself back using her spear to help, since her wounds were slowing her. Puck's claws slammed into the solid stone up to his first knuckles. With a battle cry, Ferra plunged the spear into the center of the oversized hand and vaulted upward toward his head. She tried not to smile when Puck screamed out in agony as his hand began to freeze from the wound outward. Running up his forearm, she vaulted off straight toward him, both her hands reaching for the bulbous troll head that Puck had adopted.

Skin like stone or not, there are few creatures that will not react violently when their eyes are attacked. All Puck could see was the snarling face of the ice warrior as she sailed the distance from his arm to his face, her hands ready to rip his vulnerable eyes out the second she made contact. The changeling reared himself backward, trying to avoid her attack.

The cavern was filled with the cracking sound as Puck ripped his own frozen arm in half, tumbling backward.

All he knew was pain as he fell to his back. The warrior woman thudded onto his chest half a second later. She carried no weapon but she raised her hand skyward, pantomiming the motions she would have made if she were to stab downward with her spear. As her hands came down, his eyes widened in outright fear. He saw a shard of ice form between her hands and then expand into another spear. Puck realized too late that her ice powers did not reside in the spear.

They resided in *her*.

Out of pure panic, his form dissipated into smoke as her new spear slammed into the ground uselessly. She growled as he moved toward his severed arm, still frozen behind her. The smoke became something thicker as he reabsorbed the mass into himself. "I don't know who you are," Puck's voice threatened from the coalescing creature. "But you have earned your own death."

Ferra glared back at the trickster, not a glimmer of fear in her expression. "We all earn our own death," she spat. "Come get yours." She gestured with her spear, urging him to attack her.

Puck transformed into a swarm of black bees and attacked. Unmoved, Ferra gripped her spear and waited. Halfway to her, he shifted into a blue-white flame. When the unbearable heat hit her face like a solid wall, she felt a brief stab of dread. She staggered back half a step, waiting for the flame to engulf her.

What she missed was Ruber's field surrounded the flaming mass entirely.

The orb of light flickered as the gem struggled to keep the field intact from several yards away. A face formed in the flames and Puck glared at Ruber, the eyes glowing malevolently as the mouth moved, warning the ruby that his field would not hold him, Puck, for long. Puck's words never reached Ruber since the container the ruby had created was airtight. If they had, the elemental would have responded that he didn't need to keep the field up for long.

Just long enough for the flames to burn out what little oxygen had been trapped inside the magical barrier.

Without air, the flames died as quickly as they had appeared. But in this case, these weren't normal flames but the entity Puck had become. The changeling reverted back to his true form against his will and without warning: in a word, Puck went into shock. He slammed against the containment field, shattering it and crashing violently to the ground.

Ferra lost no time in pouncing on the hapless shape-shifter.

"Ready for the death *you've* earned, little man?" The spear point moved under his chin, freezing his entire mouth shut.

"Do you have him?" Ruber asked weakly, still lying on the floor.

Without ever taking her eyes off of Puck, she replied in a weary voice, "No."

A pillar of light exploded from the altar, engulfing the bodies of both boys in a brilliance that rivaled the sun itself for a few seconds.

Which was, of course, just enough time for Puck to make his move.

I/HE plunges his/my sword into his/my chest.

I'm/he's reminded of the first time we met and he/I did the same to him.

We were connected at that point, neither one of us truly understanding what that action meant.

I/he looks down at him/me and I/he can see our entire future spread out before us.

I/he hardly knows him/me yet it feels as if we've known each other our entire lives.

He's/I'm dying, and that makes me/him sad because we thought there was more time.

There is never enough time.

He/I feel myself slipping away and my/his voice comes from farther and farther off until it is impossible for him/me to hear the words. But I/he knows what they are, because he's/I'm saying them back.

He/I loves me/you too.

I/he wonders if his/my mother will cry when she discovers his/my death.

"No one is dying," I/he says.

He/I realize that I'm/he's coming after him/me.

He/I try to wave me/him away, but it is no use. Like a skydiver/owl riding the air currents down, my/his soul slams into his/mine.

And for a moment we are one.

"That's what a Kardasian is?" I ask him as our memories begin to blur.

"I would have made a passable pleasuring," I scream as our memories continue to merge.

I see myself stabbing him though his memories, and I smile as I feel the attraction he had even as he thought he was dying.

I feel the way he felt self-conscious for the first time in his life as he looked for a shirt to put on after I had barged into the house he, Ruber, and Spike were squatting in.

I feel the warmth of my hand as I take his in the movie theater.

I feel the terror in his mind as he grabs my hand, wondering if I am going to reject him.

“Why would I reject you?” I ask him, shocked that he would think anyone would ever reject him. And in that second I have my answer. He is Hawk’keen Maragold, heir to the throne of Arcadia, and before he came to Athens, he assumed everyone would desire him. After all, he was, in Faern terms, perfect in every way. He was raised as such, and there wasn’t a man or woman alive who would dare spurn his advances.

And then he had met me.

“You are like no one I have ever met,” he says with a small smile. “You unnerve me.”

I smile back even though we are pure thought instead of flesh and blood at the moment. So the smile comes across like a beam of light that frames his face in a way that fashion models have dreamt of since the invention of the camera. It wasn’t his looks. Well, okay, at first it was all his looks, but it was more now. The core of him, his heart, is more attractive than anything the eyes could see. He wasn’t arrogant or certain he knew everything. The truth was just the opposite, in fact. He knew there was so much he didn’t know, yet he had faith that things would work out the way he thought they should. Faith that the universe in general was a good and just place and if it wasn’t, he’d work to make sure it became so.

How can you not love a man who is willing to literally force the universe to be a better place?

“That’s not me,” he whispered, his voice weaker than it had been before.

We were as far down as we could go. We had plummeted into the depths of wherever we were and the darkness around us lurked just beyond us the same way a vulture follows a lone man stumbling his last steps across a desert. It was patient and knew that sooner or later it would be fed. I looked into the abyss and, for a second, I felt a wave of nausea move through me as I realized how far down we were and how fast the end was coming up at us.

"All of that," Hawk said in a whisper. "Everything you just said wasn't me," he repeated, grabbing my attention. "That was what I thought of you."

His form was becoming transparent in front of my eyes while mine remained solid as ever. I had no idea what that signified, but he did, which meant in this weird place I did a second later.

He was dying.

I saw the wistful smile on his face as he began to take on the quality of fog. "I wish we had more time," I heard him think as his eyes slowly closed.

There was no way I could let him die. I know that sounds like an extreme reaction to a guy I had just barely met, but this wasn't just about him. I wouldn't have let a stranger die like this. The fact I had a connection to him made the thought of him dying even more repulsive. I knew him, knew him as well as I knew myself, and he didn't deserve to die, especially not in this way.

And I wasn't sure how I could live if he died.

Without a moment's hesitation I threw myself into him, not sure what I was going to do but pretty sure I couldn't make it worse. As I merged into him, I prayed silently. "Please, God, do not make this worse."

Where Hawk was supposed to be felt like a swirling mass of nothing collapsing upon itself, trying to take everything that was near with it. Without a second thought, I jumped into the hole in the center.

It wasn't until I felt myself completely swallowed by the hole that I wondered if my jumping had been the best idea.

THERE are a few things about djinn that should be clarified before we continue.

All members of the efreet family originate from Masaut'wa, the realm of fire and heat, and are widely considered some of the most powerful mortal creatures in existence. Forged from the primal matter of their realm, they are the elemental equivalent of angels for their worlds. Their powers are connected to the very fabric of reality, so it is easy to mistake what they can do as fulfilling wishes.

Djinn do not grant wishes.

Because they are higher beings, they are ruled by a series of laws and codes that seem strange and confusing to humans but are necessary for them to coexist with the rest of reality. It is these laws and their behavior under them that the rest of the nine worlds know them by.

If one knows a djinn's true name, that person may bind it in a container; the popular choices seem to be lamps and bottles.

Once captured, the djinn can be summoned and must follow the directive of the one who has called it. Because they are unwilling partners in this exchange, they usually follow the command to the very letter.

If someone summons a djinn and commands it to do something, it is vitally important that the command concludes by ordering the djinn to return to its container. Otherwise, it is freed.

Once released from their servitude, they are known for wreaking revenge on the ones who bound them in the first place. And, virtually every time they are released, a formerly enslaved djinn will turn on whomever is nearby, even if the person is not the one who initially bound him.

In rare instances, if captured, a djinn can be bound to a container and given a preset list of commands to perform when released.

Most of these facts were not known to Trias as he read the words on the scroll. Even if they had been, he could not have known what had been trapped in the box. Nor would he have known the true danger that opening and reading the parchment would entail.

All the matchstick man knew was that once he began to read the commands, he couldn't stop, and once released, the djinn that emerged was so filled with fury that there was only a snap of pain before Trias was incinerated where he stood.

Four seconds later, the tent exploded in fire.

OBERON and his guards were doing well when there was an explosion behind enemy lines.

With a burst of heated air like the wind coming off the desert plains, an unmistakable wave of power passed over both armies. Everyone froze as a roar thundered over the horizon, sending a chill up the assembled spines.

"What in the nine worlds…?" Oberon asked out loud, his sword still raised over the groveling goblin beneath him.

The first yell of the djinn sent everyone in the courtyard into a panic.

The royal guards began to fall back to the palace, but when the first two of their number were reduced to ash, the rest turned tail and ran. Oberon took a few hesitant steps back as the head of the being loomed over the crystal walls, its demonic face glaring down, an angry lord surveying all that has displeased him.

"*Fall back!*" Oberon bellowed before he sprinted to the castle proper. His words fell on deaf ears as his well-disciplined troops began to scream in terror when the djinn destroyed indiscriminately on its lumbering advance toward the palace.

By the time Oberon and most of the guards reached the castle doors, Titania was standing, aloof and calm, on the topmost step. Without sparing a glance at her consort, she commanded, "Get inside and lead everyone to the lower levels." Another portion of the crystal wall shattered under the djinn's fists, scattering shards as sharp as knives in all directions. Unmoved, Titania waited until the last scream of anyone skewered by the shards had faded. Then she darted a glance at her husband and added, "I have this."

He hesitated for half a second before the sound of more shattering crystal motivated him to heed Titania's orders and run into the palace.

If Titania had noticed her husband beating a hasty retreat, she didn't give any indication; her entire attention was directed at the djinn.

Goblins and fairies alike tried to escape the fiery rain that began to descend from the skies, but it was no use. The blood-red being took delight in killing each and every one of them with the same relish of a young child burning ants with a magnifying glass. It wasn't until it entered the courtyard proper that it noticed the queen standing there, waiting.

With a flicker of its hand, the djinn transformed the air around Titania into living flame, engulfing her entirely.

Titania moved to the offensive and, with a mere thought, converted the fire to air once again.

No word did she speak, but Titania had summoned the Taku wind, which staggered the djinn where it stood. On the back of the Taku, storm clouds built and filled the sky. Arms raised, her hands facing palms outward in denial, Titania spoke her legacy and her defiance. "I am Queen Maryrose Seelie Titania Perficio and am the lawful ruler of this and the other eight worlds by Right of Ascension. I control the *Universitas Nemus*. This is the only chance you have to escape this realm with your life."

The djinn peered at her, a lewd grin spreading across its face. "I know you, fairy queen. I know you all too well." Its voice condescending, it wagged one finger at her. "And I know your history. I know what your kind have done to achieve what you wish to believe is yours by right."

Titania's eyes darkened as the words hit home. "Silence," she commanded. Gaze never leaving the menace in front of her, she used her hands to create an intricate pattern of light and color in the air. Immediately, the djinn moved to counter the flood-spell she wove, allowing her time to complete a verbal enchantment. A steel plate slammed over the djinn's mouth, four bolts securing it shut. The sham light-spell disintegrated in a shower of sparks that helped rivet the plate permanently. The angered efreet tried to pry it off to no avail.

All the while the Taku blew, and the air around it chilled more rapidly as Titania's spell took effect. She was opening a portal to Niflgard, home of the ice giants. Its kind would perish there almost instantly and she knew it. Faced with certain destruction, the djinn summoned heat before the air froze around it. Its hands glowed as it directed its hottest fires to its palms. Within seconds, the heat was so intense its palms shone blue-white. Behind it, the portal had opened a crack and widened by the second. It placed both hands against the metal plate.

The only fire that burns hotter than a djinn's makes its home in the forges of Djupur Byrjun and is constantly tended by the dwarves of Kh'zdule. There is no substance known to man or Faerth able to withstand the full heat of the djinn. Titania's magical steel was no exception. Slowly, it melted, oozing down the chin of the monster.

Unaffected by the molten substance, the efreet thrust its arms out wide, calling upon the power of *Elohim*, creator of all. Titania's portal was shattered by the harsh desert winds that issued forth from its hands. The fairy queen could feel the heat from where she stood, what felt like a wall of fire raging toward her.

Furrowing her brow, she focused for a second before letting out one continuous breath of air. The heat broke almost instantly when her cold wave hit the djinn's barrier. Steam exploded around them as the two temperatures met head-on, and the entire courtyard was obscured for a precious few seconds.

Seconds the djinn took advantage of.

Unaffected by the superheated steam, it focused its powers on the ground where the accursed queen stood. The stone turned to lava almost instantly as the front steps collapsed into the growing pool of molten stone. "I was ordered to destroy you, your highness; I cannot leave until that is done," it said conversationally, more to itself than to the recently deceased ruler.

"I apologize for being harder to kill than you expected, then," Titania replied from behind it. The djinn wheeled to face her but was already too late. She raised her hands, controlling the storm clouds above. Thunder cracked across the land as a bolt of lightning wider than a house struck the creature in the center of its head. Although blinded, the efreet roared a word of command, uncreating the storm from the inside out. The skies lightened instantly as the clouds rolled backward into nothing.

"I have walked the bowels of Djupur Byrjun itself, my dear fairy! Do you hope me affected by mere lightning?"

"No," she answered as the djinn's vision slowly returned. She stood in front of it, her arms still skyward, seemingly still controlling the storm that was no longer there. "I simply needed you unaware for a moment."

Speaking another word of command, the djinn protected itself from all forms of arcane assault. "And what did that achieve?" it mocked. "Your storm is gone, in case you didn't notice."

A small smile appeared on her face. "I know. I was directing the lava."

The djinn saw the flash of red from the corner of its eye as the entire mass of lava came crashing around it, grabbing it like a fist. It laughed as it looked back at her. "You cannot burn me, foolish girl!"

Her smile widened. "I know."

With another word, she called down another arctic burst of wind.

The lava went from molten to solid in seconds, encasing the djinn from its neck down. It tried to move its arms; however, the lava itself was not magical, so its protection had no effect on it. It opened its mouth to speak a third word of command, but Titania was quicker. She cast another spell, simply spoken, old as time, and part and parcel of the earth she stood upon. The stone prison encasing the djinn grumbled a bit as its roots sank deep into the earth and its substance was cemented by a binding spell.

The djinn's eyes widened in horror as it realized it had just been recaptured.

"Now, shall we try this again?" she said, mocking its arrogant tone back to it. "I am Queen Maryrose Seelie Titania Perficio and am the lawful ruler of this and the other eight worlds by Right of Ascension. I control the *Universitas Nemus,* and your life now belongs to me."

The creature snarled at her as it futilely tried to escape. Its kind was all-powerful, but there were laws, and the laws stated that if captured, it was bound to her will. Its only saving grace was the fact it remained bound to a previous set of commands.

"I was ordered to destroy you, and destroy you I shall," it said proudly, its eyes flashing with fury. "What your kind has done to achieve power was a crime against the nine worlds. Your time of reckoning is coming, dear Titania. The roots of your realm are rotten, and it begins to wither from within. There is only one who can save you now. I tell you this freely and of my own will." It leaned as far forward as it could to make its point. "No matter the outcome, your son will die for your sins. Only with his blood will the scales be balanced and the Tree be made whole again. Look into my eyes, fairy, and see the truth. Your son is already dead. He simply hasn't stopped moving yet."

Titania saw a vision in the djinn's eyes and her face paled in horror.

"And with that," it said smugly, "you are destroyed."

There was nothing she could say in response, because she knew it was right.

FERRA wheeled toward the explosion of light, wondering if it was some kind of new attack. She looked up in amazement as Hawk floated above the altar, Kane unconscious in his arms. They were both surrounded by a nimbus of golden light that radiated power, which she could feel even from across the room.

The look on the fairy's face was as beautiful as it was terrifying. The raw fury that was etched in those perfect features made him more like the statue of an angry demigod than an actual flesh-and-blood being. Though she had no idea who the boy was, it was obvious to the Frigus that he was not someone she wanted against her.

Before she could finish the thought, her lower back exploded in pain as Puck slashed her, the fingers of his hand replaced by five short sword blades.

She instantly fell to the ground, her legs no longer responding to her brain's commands. Not until she realized she couldn't feel the cold stone floor did she know that something had gone drastically wrong. Pain meant damaged but working body functions; nothing meant death. Ferra lay there, unable to move as Puck stepped over her toward Hawk.

"So, the slumbering prince is awakened by the kiss of a princess. That's a twist." His voice was mocking and condescending, but his eyes were still alive with caution. "Have enough people been killed, or do you need a larger body count before you will surrender the secret of Ascension?"

Hawk said nothing as he pointed the tip of his sword at the changeling. They locked eyes for what seemed to be forever before the prince, in a voice that echoed throughout the Dark, spoke one only word.

"Die."

Bolts of power shot out from Truheart, forcing the changeling to scramble this way and that to keep whole. Everywhere he dodged, Puck met another bolt that burst in front of him, forcing him to reverse his position with a half twist or risk being hit by the arcane power.

Even as he danced with his own death, Puck's always busy mind wondered how the prince had learned to summon and control such powerful forces. The boy was no 'Caster; his only natural affinity had been with sword dancing, and even then he was considered a marginal student. The power he commanded now far exceeded anything in Puck's experience. He hit the floor of the cave as a bolt blazed through the spot where he'd been standing upright. Dimly Puck realized that the force hurled at him was growing, and he was running out of places to dodge.

HIS mind still reeling from having his shield shattered so violently, Ruber forced himself to focus on the chamber. Kane had passed through his force field as if it hadn't existed, and the blowback had been akin to a full-frontal assault on the elemental. But he could see Hawk floating there, barraging Puck with some kind of magical energy. Not magical energy—

The walls of the cave were blackened from missed strikes, the floor filled with small holes from the bolts that had pocked it. That was life force!

"Hawk!" he cried out, wobbling into the air like a hatchling bird on its first flight. "Prince Hawk! Stop!" But his words fell on deaf ears. Knowing he had no other choice, Ruber floated up to Hawk, diving into the prince's face.

"*You must stop!*" the ruby screamed, concentrating as much energy as he could into a burst of light without causing himself or Hawk permanent harm.

Hawk flinched away from the flash and his concentration broke for a split second. The bolts stopped for that same breath of time. In the sudden silence, Ruber saw Hawk's glowing eyes turn toward him, their unbridled wrath now focused on him. There was no recognition in Hawk's eyes now, only anger and power.

"You're killing him!" Ruber continued quickly, before Hawk's attention could return to slaying Puck. "You're draining his life force!" Hawk's expression shifted slightly toward puzzlement. He had no idea what Ruber was talking about. Before the prince could return to Puck's destruction, the elemental pressed on. "Kane! You're killing Kane!"

The name dragged Hawk from the depths of his berserk rage, and he looked down at the human in his arms. Kane's face was gaunt and pale, as if he had not eaten in weeks. His limbs hung as if they were boneless, making him look more dead than unconscious. Seeing Kane in such a state, and understanding the fact that he had almost killed him, brought Hawk out of his rage instantly. The glow vanished and he fell to the ground, bracing Kane's fall with his own body.

Ruber sighed metaphorically and dropped slowly until he floated where the two boys lay motionless. He could see Ferra lying there as well, a pool of blood forming underneath her. But—Ruber scanned the room quickly, but his worst fears were realized.

Puck had escaped.

"We don't have a lot of time," he said aloud, not sure where to begin. He floated to Ferra and then back to the boys, knowing he lacked the resources to heal all of them.

"Fix. The. Boy." Ferra choked, her breath coming in ragged gasps as she forced herself to keep breathing.

"I'm not sure I can," Ruber responded quietly. He examined Kane and Hawk using a ruby gem elemental's equivalent of a CAT scan. What he found was not in the least promising.

"I do believe that they are…," he began to explain to Ferra, trying to keep her attention on him and not on dying, when two dark elves burst into the room.

They were the two assassins who had attacked Hawk back on Earth.

In a burst of speed, Ruber placed himself between the two elves and the boys, forcing himself to glow as brightly as possible, hoping to bluff the elves. "These people are under my protection. Harm them at your own peril," he threatened.

"I told you they could not be trusted," Pullus grumbled at Ater. The dark elf was obviously continuing the conversation he and Ater had been engaged in before their abrupt arrival in the nyxies' ruined cave.

Ater held in a sigh and continued to watch the ruby. "Later. Deal with this now." Both elves had their weapons drawn but neither one brought them up for attack.

"We do not mean the prince any harm," Ater said quietly.

"Says the assassin who tried to kill him," Ruber countered.

"He has a point," Pullus commented.

Ater looked over at him, shooting him a deathly glare. Turning back to Ruber, he said in a controlled tone, "If I wished him dead, he would be dead."

"*That's* the tack you're going to take?" Pullus exclaimed. "We could have killed him but didn't, so trust us?"

Ater sighed, looking back to his partner again. "Well then, how would *you* convince him our intentions aren't hostile?"

Pullus shrugged and gestured to the door behind him. "How about 'We're being cornered by the mob Puck has gathered. He's told them that he's found the ones responsible for the slaughter of their families, and they're headed this way right now'? How about that one?"

Ater glanced over his shoulder at the door and listened for a second. Although still barely audible, the sound of an angry mob on the hunt was growing louder. Looking back at Ruber, he said quickly, "He's right, we need to leave!"

Ruber didn't move. "One, I am not convinced that anything you have said is the truth, and two, this is the heir to the throne of Arcadia. No one from The Under would dare touch him."

"The Dark attacked the palace less than an hour ago," Ater stated grimly. "He's not the heir to anything right now. However, he *will* be the bargaining chip they use to force the royal family to surrender. We have to leave!"

Ruber looked to the boys who still lay, unmoving, on the floor, and to Ferra, who was slowly bleeding out as they argued.

The mob was getting closer.

"Dammit," Ruber snapped. Repositioning himself over Hawk and Kane, he ordered, "Well, get closer. If this is to have any chance of working, we need to be as close as possible. Move her," bobbing toward Ferra, "as gently as you can." Without hesitation, Ater pointed Pullus over close to Kane, then pushed Ferra as carefully as he could manage toward Ruber.

"Where are you taking us?" Pullus asked with more curiosity than concern.

"The only place I can manage to transport this many people to in my condition." Ruber again focused his glow, this time bathing everyone in the light. Hawk shifted when the ground, softened by Ruber's magics, became malleable and permeable. As one, they began to sink slowly into it. "Home."

Within seconds, they had sunk into the ground, leaving no trace they had ever been there.

Interlude One

BY the time Puck had convinced enough creatures that the ones responsible for attacking the marketplace were cornered in the nyxies' cave, it was too late. The chamber stood empty when his makeshift army burst through the doorway. Copious amounts of fresh blood staining the stone floor were the only indication that anyone had ever been there.

Shifting his eyes slightly, the changeling could see the arcane traces of a dimensional shift just in front of the altar. The russet-brown color of the residue signified that the teleportation's terminal lay in a physically deeper plane of existence. Since without a facilitation spell, the human world was cut off from the nine worlds, the only place the gem could take them was the plane of Earth, a place to which Puck had no access.

The damned ruby had taken with him Puck's only chance at Ascension.

"This is getting tiresome," he grumbled to himself as he slowly backed out of the mob and began to make his way to the surface after morphing into a shadow. His entire plan hinged on being able to Ascend once he had been made ruler of Arcadia; without that final step, he would be an empty dictator at best. Only an Ascended One could command the power of the nine worlds, and only with power could Puck make his murderous dreams come true.

He had hoped to use the boy as leverage against Titania; perhaps it was time to rethink this plan. If he couldn't get to Hawk, then he would need to find a way to get Hawk to come to him.

"*Oberon,*" he said in a moment of epiphany.

Once clear of The Under, Puck became a deerhound and loped swiftly toward the palace, knowing exactly what he needed to do next.

Interlude Two

THE king could see his wife was distressed when she returned to the palace.

He was her legally bound consort; however, Titania had, by Ascending, won the power to rule the Nine Worlds. She didn't share power, a fact which Oberon never forgot and Titania never failed to remind him of. Discontented though he might be in private, in public Oberon supported the queen in all she did. Because of her, they had enjoyed almost two thousand years of peace with the other realms, a fact she never let *anyone* else forget.

However, the fight with the djinn had shaken her somehow, and not physically. It was the first sign of weakness he had seen in the queen since they had wed so many years before. There was a hesitancy in her eyes, an uncertainty that in no way spoke of perfection. To an outsider, she simply appeared agitated, possibly shaken up by the fight.

Not to him.

Not to the one who had spent countless centuries looking for one small chink in that impenetrable armor she wore around her heart. She had put down insurgencies before, and he had seen her do it with a zealous glee that made him think twice before hatching his own plan to dethrone his wife. But now, whatever had occurred during Titania's battle with the djinn had broken through her defenses and left her ever so slightly vulnerable. Oberon caught a glimpse of the Faerth she had been before the desire for Ascension had taken control of her. Inside himself, he smiled broadly.

"Are you well?" he asked, his voice full of genuine-sounding concern. He stepped closer to take her arm to assist her but she waved him off.

"He knows," she responded, her voice obviously distracted. "The damned thing knew how Faerth became the center of the nine worlds."

Though troubling, Titania's revelation wasn't very surprising to Oberon. After all, djinns were Higher Powers in their own realm. It would have been impossible to keep what the Faerth and Titania had done hidden from those who were attuned to the way the universe worked. Most of the beings who knew the truth had little concern as to the precise location of the center of the nine worlds; they demanded only that it exist somewhere. Further, no being in any realm had complained when the Faerth had sealed the human world off from the rest of the realms. In Oberon's opinion, their lack of response implied apathy toward Faerth and Titania's actions, if not outright consent.

"And?" he asked when she didn't continue. "Did he threaten to expose the truth?"

She said nothing until they were safely in her private chambers. When she turned to him, he saw the abject fear in her eyes as she replied, "No. He said that Hawk was going to pay for what we had done. He showed me Hawk, and he was dying. He is dying right now."

Oberon stared at her for several seconds, his eyes blinking. When it became obvious she wanted a response from him, he uttered only one word to her. "And?"

It was the wrong word.

"And?" she echoed. "*And—*" This time a roar. "Our son is dying because of what we did to gain power, and all you can say is *and*?" The sound of thunder echoed through the castle as her power voiced her fury.

"Your son," he replied after a second of silence. "Your son, not mine."

"And whose fault is that?" she hissed back at him.

"What you did is your own business." He shrugged, completely unimpressed by her anger. "But it is not what *we* did but what *you* did to gain power." He gave her a small smile. "I, as you are fond of reminding me, have no actual power."

Had he slapped her across the face, he would have gotten the same reaction from her. She was frozen in outrage and disbelief at her husband's indifference to their son's fate. "You don't care about Hawk." She wasn't asking; she was stating the fact as the truth dawned on her.

"What I care about has always been of little concern to you. I'm not sure why you would care now. No, I don't care about Hawk." His words were as cruel as he could make them while he tried to exploit her sudden emotional vulnerability. "Besides, I'm not going to be the one responsible for his death, am I?"

She said nothing for several seconds, the only sound in the room coming from the dying embers in the fireplace. "Make yourself useful for once," she said, waving her right hand in dismissal as she turned away. "Be a dear and tell the steward the fire needs tending." No one could have measured the amount of control she exerted to make her tone casually unresponsive. And Oberon hadn't the finesse to see it.

He gave her a mocking little half bow as he backed of the room. "As you wish." But he knew that he'd been bettered somehow so the bow was taut and short, the words poorly spoken.

Only after the door had closed behind him did Titania react. One word and a sharp chop of the hand and the door disappeared, leaving a smooth plaster-covered brick wall in its place. Only when she was sure that she was alone and couldn't be heard did she allow herself to weep aloud.

Oberon stood on the other side of the wall. For a few seconds anger ruled him, but then a thought occurred and an ever-wider smile lit his face as he realized what he needed to do next.

CHAPTER NINE

"The Gnome King had always been a source of great conflict in Djupur Byrjun. His greed was only matched by his great desire to rule."
An Overview for the Crystal Court, Caerus Decor Silentium

THE relationship between the dwarven kingdom of Kh'zdule and the Gnome King had always been tenuous.

The Gnome King claimed that the domain of everything under the ground was his and that to trespass on his holding constituted a declaration of war. The dwarves of Kh'zdule made their living mining the precious minerals that were only found beneath the crust of Djupur Byrjun. Because the Gnome King could not be everywhere, the dwarves had operated virtually untouched for the past seven thousand years, with only minor skirmishes here and there when the two met.

This all changed when Faerth became the center of the nine realms.

For reasons unknown to the subterranean dwellers, when the fairies took control of the nine worlds and exiled Earth, everything changed for the worse. The resources they mined became scarcer and scarcer, until the dwarves were forced to strike out to find new nodes of the minerals that kept their society prosperous and thriving. This meant willingly entering lands that were occupied by the Gnome King and his subjects, and that meant war.

Never ones to shy away from a battle, the dwarves met the Gnome King's stone army head-on, making the strip of land where the two kingdoms abutted a war zone for all involved. Vast amounts of arcane energies were required by the Gnome King to keep his unliving army in motion. Additionally, the dwarves mined and sold the minerals they retrieved in order to survive; because they were living beings and vulnerable, they used guerrilla tactics to keep the Gnome army at bay as they sought and extracted the metals they required. What had started as a full battle had slowed to a cold war of attrition. The situation remained unresolved. At best, the dwarves and the gnomes maintained a tenuous truce, resting on a powder keg of hostility which threatened to explode at the least provocation.

The difference lay in which side the Crystal Court decided to ally itself with.

Made up of the totality of gem elementals that were only to be found in Djupur Byrjun, the Crystal Court had little use for the endless quarrels the other inhabitants of the world seemed to thrive on. Led by Lord Adamas, First Diamond to the Djupur, they had been approached by both sides with offers of alliance, each one offering the gems wealth and power beyond their imagination. Not wishing to rush the decision, the Court had decided to withdraw from the surface world to ponder its choices.

That had been approximately four and a half centuries ago.

Since then, the Crystal Court had become more and more isolated, until it was virtually forgotten by both sides. Hidden in the deepest strata of the Evrose Mountains, the Court lived in relative peace compared to the constant state of hostilities that lay just outside and above its door.

So a group of flesh beings falling through the ceiling onto the floor of the Main Library caused quite a stir.

Two amber guards froze in midair and stared in outright shock as Ater and Pullus struggled to their feet. Both dark elves stumbled and grabbed for each other as they tried to shake off the dimensional jump. Ruber, who wobbled erratically just above and beyond the two, looked at the two smooth oval gems and barked out a booming "*Get someone*!" which immediately shattered both the gem elementals' stupor. They flew out of the room without a word, leaving the newly arrived group alone.

"Not even stones," Ruber mused, his inner glow almost completely out as he tumbled unceremoniously to the floor.

"That's not good," Pullus said, not making a move toward the downed ruby.

"Where are we?" Ater asked, looking around in poorly disguised awe. The room that surrounded them was massive. The entire ceiling had been created from one huge piece of quartz that had been intricately carved in an endless display of geometrical patterns. Scores of shelves were carved out of one seamless piece of stone. They held hundreds of thousands of gem plates carved to look like books made of oversized jewels. Just one of the "books" would be priceless in Faerth. The assembled value of all of them was immeasurable.

Pullus looked around the room. "I would assume these would be books for gem elementals, which would make this a library of sorts?"

"Close," Ruber said in a tired voice. "It is the collected knowledge of our race, preserved in a static form for easy retrieval."

The two dark elves looked at each other for a moment. "So, books," Ater clarified.

Before Ruber could answer, the double doors burst open, revealing a square, iridescent pink gem a little smaller than Ruber, flanked by two dozen smooth oval pieces of amber. Neither dark elf moved as the pink sapphire left its cordon of guards to float closer to Ruber.

"Raatnaraj?" it asked in a decidedly female voice. "Raatnaraj Ruber Scientia, what are you doing on the floor? And who are these people?"

"I am on the floor because I am in pain, Caerus. These people are with me," he answered in a tone that sounded like he was trying to keep the annoyance out of his voice and failing miserably.

"I thought you were going," she said, ignoring the pile of unconscious humans behind him. "Father said you had left this realm."

Now the weariness and irritation was impossible to miss in the ruby's voice. "I have been gone for 3,100 years, sister!"

She floated there, her emotions, if indeed she had any, unreadable to the two dark elves. After a moment of contemplation, she asked, "So then, it was just a visit?"

Ruber's glow finally gave out as he sighed in exhaustion. The world went black.

WHEN I woke up....

You know what? I am sick of saying that. There is something certain fantasy stories do not prepare you for and, since I seem to be stuck in the middle of one, I feel I should comment on it. There is a four-eyed, facially scarred wizard who goes on and on about all the things that are *fun*. This is him on a broomstick, this is him getting drunk at an underage bar, this is him one step away from being a perv wandering the halls under an invisibility cloak. Sure you hear all that, and that's great, but how many copies of Stupid Kid Wizard and the Weekend He Lost From Being Hit On the Head Too Much do you think people would buy?

Though if it were written, I would probably be standing in line at midnight with Jewel in front of Lucien's library, dressed in robes, waiting to snag a copy.

Either way, as an average person in the middle of nine realms of chaos, I seem to have spent more than my share of time passed out and waking up somewhere strange. If I'm being honest, I've actually spent my share and a few more people's shares as well. The long and the short of what I'm getting at is this: if you go off chasing rabbits and you know you're going to go headfirst down an oversized rabbit hole, wear some pads, because adventuring is a full-contact sport.

Where was I?

Oh yeah, so when I woke up, I found myself face-to-face with a floating emerald the size of a soda can. You'd think by now I would be immune to this kind of thing, but no dice. I still screamed like a little girl seeing Zac Efron in the mall. The emerald shot backward when I tried to kick the sheets off my lower body. Unsuccessfully, since they weighed more than I did. This time I was in a bed. Which wasn't quite right, since this bed was like the king of all beds. You know the kind of bed that looks over-the-top? With the four posts and the draping sheet on the top with frilly stuff all over everywhere else, not to mention twelve pillows in different sizes, kind of like if beds had drag queens, those kinds of beds?

Those kinds of beds *wish* they were as fabulous as this bed was.

I tried to back away from the floating green rectangle, but moving on that mattress was like trying to find traction in quicksand. And the sheets still pretty effectively kept me trapped. I got caught up in the sheets, more sheets, blanket, and what I assumed was a duvet. I was trying to get away from a piece of gravity-challenged rock, so for all I knew I had been trapped by a giant bed monster and had awakened midway through lunch.

I'm rambling.

My mind isn't the fastest runner in the race, but it gets there. Since I'd been hanging out with a floating ruby, it wasn't much of a stretch to reason a floating emerald might be similar. Forcing down the panic that accompanied yet again waking up with no idea where I was, I sat up and peeked over the edge of the bed. "Hello?" I called tentatively. "Are you there?"

The emerald shot up into my line of sight, bobbing slightly. "Where else would I be?" it replied in a voice that obviously belonged to a young boy. A young boy with a laughably proper English accent, but a kid nonetheless. "Did you think I dislocated? Because I can't do that yet."

If he was still scared, he didn't show it by the way he zipped toward me. "You mean teleported?" I asked as I sat fully upright.

"No. Teleporting is moving from one place to another by traveling between an inter-dimensional space that uses space and time differently than your current plane does. Dislocating is moving from one point to another using line-of-sight spatial folding." He sounded like he was reciting lessons from a book the way he fumbled over some of the more complicated words.

"Okay. Well, dislocated means you pulled a limb out of joint where I come from," I explained.

"I don't have limbs," he advised me, enunciating carefully as if I was slow.

"I see that." I tried to keep the annoyance out of my voice.

"So I can't pull one from anywhere," he added.

"I get that."

"So then, it can't mean here what it means where you come from," he concluded proudly. To me, his words sounded like nonsense, but as with all kids, what he said made perfect sense to him.

"Okay, well, now I know," I agreed. I took a breath and made sure I had wriggled clear of the sheets before I made the trek to the edge of the bed again. I'm pretty sure the thing had its own zip code, it was so big. "So what's your name?" I asked as I absorbed the fact I was so high up, there was literally a drop-off to the floor. I started feeling dizzy. I'd never been afraid of heights before, but I was pretty sure I'd turned the corner on that as well.

"I am Lates Discipulus of the Crystal Court," he replied.

"You're related to Ruber?" I asked, contemplating making a rope out of the pillow cases to get down.

"Who's Ruber?" he asked, obviously not noticing the trouble I was having dismounting my beast of a bed.

"Um," I said as I struggled to remember Ruber's full title. "Ratface Ruber Sciencesomething or other?"

The little emerald gasped as it recoiled back a few feet. "His name is Raatnaraj Ruber Scientia, and he's my big brother!" He sounded as insulted as Ruber would have if he'd heard me mess up his name that badly.

"Sorry." I tried to calm him down. "But his middle name is Ruber, right?"

I really thought the emerald was going to explode, it was so pissed off. "We do not refer to adults by their middle name once they become elders!"

I decided not to push that. "I call him Ruber. So you're Lates?" I asked, doing my best to pronounce the kid's name correctly. The "a" sounded like the "a" in "lap" more than the "a" in "latte." Is that a word? Jewel would have let me play it in Scrabble, so it must be.

"Lates Discipulus," he said, emphasizing the second name gravely.

"What's your third name? Or is it the same as Ruber's?" I asked as I hefted one of the pillows over the side and let it plummet to the floor. The pillows were, by the way, proportional to the bed; I never knew feathers could end up being heavy.

"Raatnaraj Ruber Scientia has earned all three of his titles. I have not obtained my third yet." In a low voice, he added, "I barely got my second."

"What do they all mean?" I asked as I rolled another pillow over and down. "I mean, where I come from, our parents just name us. You make it sound like names are more important here."

He flew closer to me, which I took as him leaning in to make a point. "Names are everything!" he exclaimed in the same tone a kid from Earth would use if you said you didn't like candy or something. "You are given your first name once you are formed. Your second name is determined by your sire to define your attitude, and you choose your third name to represent what you strive for. When the time is right, you switch the first and second names to show you are independent of your family. That's why the second name is never used again, because it would be calling someone a child!" From the tone of his voice, I was pretty sure I'd just been chastised. "Also, I didn't mean 'you' when I said 'you', of course."

I sat there and tried to sort out what Lates had said, but it just sounded like the hokey pokey to me. "Okay. So explain Ruber's name to me," I said, working up the courage to jump off the bed.

"Ruber is his classification, since he is a ruby," Lates began, sounding just like a little kid does when he knows something and is inordinately proud of explaining it. "He was given that name at forming. The second, Raatnaraj, was given to him by our father. And the third, Scientia, was the life path he chose."

"What do the last two mean?" I asked, counting in my head to three, then six, and finally deciding that ten sounded the best. Counted slowly, very slowly.

"Scientia is the path of science and knowledge, which meant he wanted to be a seeker of the truth," Lates explained patiently. "And Raatnaraj means *king,* which signified that he was next in line to the throne."

"What?" I asked as I pushed off the bed and shot a stare at Lates at the same instant. I came down twisted sideways. I tried to digest that. Ruber was supposed to be king? The pillows, by the way, did nothing to keep my ass from hitting the stone floor hard enough to make my bones smart. The good part was I was off that mountain of a bed. "Ruber is supposed to be king?" I asked, rubbing my backside and wincing.

"I *was*," Ruber said from the door. "Lates Discipulus, what did I say about the humans?"

The emerald lost altitude a bit as it answered. "You said not to bother them, but I didn't bother them, he woke up all by himself and then he asked me a question, which I had to answer because it is only polite and as royalty we are supposed to be polite as—"

If gem elementals breathed, Lates would have been talking in one *long* one until he ran out of air. Which, of course, he never would. Ruber cut him off. "You know what I mean." His voice was strict, but he didn't sound angry, just forceful. That was a new tone from Ruber. "Go inform your sister that the humans are awake and to ask about the condition of the injured one."

Lates began to shoot out of the room, but I called out to him. "Lates! Wait!" He paused at the door, spinning around until he was staring at me. "Say 'Charlie bit my finger'."

"What?" he asked, confused. "Who is Charlie, and why would he bite your finger?"

"Lates, go," Ruber ordered. The emerald flew out of the room so fast all I saw was a streak of green. "I apologize, he's only five thousand and fourteen years old; he is still learning."

I stood up slowly. My butt was burning and—Shut up! You have a dirty mind.

"And how old are you?" I asked, trying not to fall down as I walked over the pillows.

"Too old," he said with a seriousness I had never noticed in his voice before. "Hawk is awake and asking for you. I assume you want to see him before you meet my family."

Suddenly everything flashed back into my mind and I remembered how hurt he had been. "Is he the injured one?" Even as I asked, I knew he wasn't. He was worried but not hurt, well, not any more hurt than he had been before.

"No. Ferra has been hurt, but we are attending to her. Fortunately, we have someone who is well versed in healing humans."

Tired. Ruber sounded tired, which was something new for Ruber. Annoyed, snippy, British, yes. Tired? Never.

"Are you okay?" I asked as we walked out of the room into a large hall.

"I am as well as I am going to be," he answered cryptically. When he noticed me staring at him, he clarified. "This is a place I never intended to come back to. It takes some adjusting to believe I am actually here again."

"I'm sorry," I said, trying to make him feel better. "You want to talk about it?"

He rotated toward me, and I knew for a fact he was looking right at me. "No, I don't. And I beg of you, please do not make me talk about it."

"What?" I asked, shocked. "I wouldn't make you do anything you didn't want to!"

"Well, thank you for that. Leaving here and returning are not topics I wish to discuss any time soon."

We walked in silence as he took me to another enormous door at the end of the hall. "He is in there. Once I know Ferra's condition, I will alert you."

"Ruber," I called as he started to float off. "Thank you. I mean, for everything. Really. You've been the best."

He floated down a few feet and then rose again, the gem elemental equivalent of a bow, I think. "We were in danger; I did what had to be done. There is no need to thank me."

I smiled at him. "No need, perhaps, but that doesn't mean it shouldn't be said."

He bowed again. "Thank you for that, Kane. You are more than welcome."

"How do I get down from this damned bed?" Hawk screamed from the other side of the door.

"That's my cue," I said, trying not to laugh.

FERRA woke and stared up at a woman's face, covered with a bronze mask, staring down at her.

Her mind was still fogged from her injury, so she didn't react to the face until its eyes blinked while it watched her. Then she reared away from the visage. She gripped her left hand tightly and ice began to form inside her palm. "What in the nine hells are you?" she croaked, trying to keep as much of her composure as possible. If she had to fight, Ferra knew she was beaten; the pain and exhaustion of her injuries were still too great for her to defend herself.

The brass girl took a few steps back. The only indication that she was surprised came when the metal around her eyes irised open like a camera lens, mimicking a shocked expression. "Oh! I didn't mean to startle you." Her voice was kind and emotive, just verging on the edge of being a parody of concern, but the earnestness in the way she talked seemed to give it validation. "I was just concerned about you."

Ferra let the ice fade as her nerves settled a bit. "I was injured?" she asked in confusion.

The clockwork girl nodded. "You'd lost a lot of oil, and your casing was severely damaged. But the gems have fixed you up pretty well."

Ferra's fingers traced her lower back. She swore there were slight traces of where Puck had severed her spine left on the new skin. She remembered the bolt of light and then being struck from behind but not much else. "Where am I?" she asked after a few seconds of contemplation. "And who are you?" Ferra refrained from asking what the metal creature was as well.

Molly was made in the image of a perfect human female in every detail possible, the only exception being that she was created from brass. Her eyes were made of coke-bottle-green glass placed in the center of two perfect discs of ivory. Those eyes were far more expressive than you'd think possible in a clockwork being.

She wore clothes that had been fashioned to fit her frame. Her dress, a demure shirtwaist with a hem that stopped just above her knees, had been made of pressed pieces of gold and platinum that looked as if they had once been polished to a high gloss but had lost their luster over time. Her fingertips were adorned with blood-red ovals of porcelain that, no doubt, had once resembled nails. However, they had been chipped and broken until all that was left were small pieces where the cuticle was on a human's finger. The untidy nail beds only accented her state of disrepair.

Her voice, though melodic, sounded as if it issued from an old-style gramophone that had once recorded the sound of a lovely woman speaking with perfect diction. Her hair was made of burnt silver strands, all carefully welded and fit into place as a tight bun with curls for bangs, fastened with a silver comb that looked all the brighter in her dark-black hair. She had seven small keyholes that were placed along what would have been her collarbone. Each one tightened a spring that had been designated a specific function.

Tinker and Jones Clockwork Beings, a legendary bastion of clockwork quality, had been in existence since 926 in the year of the sixth Vale. As one of their clockwork companions, Molly came with the standard three springs assigned to Thought, Action, and Speech. However, she had also been provided with four additional springs because, as a Companion, she needed the attributes they governed. The first one provided Compassion, allowing her to empathize and to feel for whomever she was told to love. Another allowed her to utilize Coquettishness, primarily for innocent flirting and conversational gambits. Next to last was Etiquette, giving her the knowledge of proper manners in almost any situation she might ever encounter. The last, for Subservience, alas, was broken beyond repair, a common occurrence in the female companion models.

Most of the time, the damage was inflicted by the clockwork women themselves.

Molly had been a gift, a proof of goodwill, from the Gnome King to the Crystal Court during initial negotiations. Ever since the dwarves had been forced to abandon Evna, the value of the few remaining clockwork beings had risen astronomically. So, although the Crystal Court had no use for a clockwork companion, the enormous value of the gesture she represented was understood by all.

Understood by all, but of absolutely no use when it came to defining what a clockwork girl might do in a realm of gem elementals.

The decision whether or not to ally with either the court of the Gnome King or with the Dwarves was one of great importance. Since making the determination would take considerable time, the likelihood that either the Gnomes or the Dwarves might make a preemptive strike against the Crystal Court to ensure its allegiance was not outside the realm of possibility. Since she did not sleep, eat, or grow tired, Molly was at first used as menial labor to fortify the court against outside intrusion. Like Molly, the elementals were not burdened with the needs of a physical body. Once they sealed the court, there was no reason for them to venture outside. After the Great Sealing of the Gates, she remained a permanent guest of Adamas, Ruber's father and king of the Crystal Court.

To be honest, Molly had been terribly bored for the past thousand years or so.

Built to be the perfect companion for human beings, her skills were lost on the gems, who seemed to neither need nor want any form of emotional expression with others. Each one was tasked with an area of expertise, and they spent their entire life gaining knowledge and then honing their skills in whatever they had chosen. Since none of them had any desire to learn human etiquette or how clockwork beings work, Molly had spent the last few hundred years wandering the court, doing everything she could to keep herself busy.

When the living beings had arrived, she was so overjoyed she almost broke a main spring. She did not, however, inform Ferra of that.

"So they healed me?" Ferra asked once Molly was done with her explanation.

The clockwork girl edged a few paces closer to the bed. "They have an amethyst who is skilled in healing humanoids." In an anxious voice she asked, "Are you better?"

The barbarian wiggled her toes and sighed in relief when she saw them move. "Much better. The changeling almost killed me. I honestly thought I was dead." Ferra was dismayed to find how little she had been worried about her own life and now how uneventful being saved from such a fate was to her.

Molly's expression instantly settled into a scornful frown; her voice sounded as dismissive as one of the Elders in Ferra's old camp. "If you were dead, you'd complain a lot less." Ferra's body stiffened in surprise as Molly covered her own mouth with both hands. The tone of her voice was muffled when she explained, "Not that I *care* what you think, but my compassion spring has run down, which means I am currently having difficulty expressing any. Compassion, that is. Please ignore anything I am saying."

Ferra watched as Molly pulled a chain around her neck free from her dress and exposed a brass key with the symbol of Tinker and Jones on top of it. The ice warrior watched as Molly inserted it into one of the keyholes on her neck and wound clockwise several times. "I apologize for my outburst; without actual humans around, I have become lax about keeping my Compassion and Coquette as tight as they should be." After thirteen seconds of winding, she moved the key into another hole. "Normally, I would never say such horrible things."

Ferra smiled a bit. "Well, if what you said was rude, it was the politest rude I've ever heard."

Molly smiled back. "I always keep my Etiquette tightly wound. The Crystal Court does insist on manners."

"Good to know," the Frigus muttered. Throwing back her covers, she attempted to get out of bed, which, unlike the ones in the guest quarters, was normal-size. "So where are my friends?"

Molly stopped in midwind and sprang toward the bed to keep Ferra still. "Oh no! You must stay still. The mending on your back is still—"

And then Ferra felt the pain return.

A searing hot poker might as well have been applied to her lower back, and she fell to the floor. She bit her bottom lip to prevent from screaming out in agony.

"Silica!" Molly called out, her voice crescendoing to rock concert decibels as she turned up her internal volume. "Come quickly!"

Within seconds a deep-purple stone charged through the air. Its form was a double helix, enclosing a central cylinder covered all over with words that spun and flowed both within it and on its surface. "I thought you were going to keep her lying down!" the healer remarked sharply. Molly lifted Ferra back onto the bed, picking up the large warrior woman as if she weighed nothing and setting her down with gentle precision.

"I had a loose spring, and she moved too quickly for me to stop her," the mechanical girl explained.

Ferra writhed in pain as the magical healing unraveled. Blood from the reopened wound soaked the bed. "She tore the sutures. Hold her down!" the gem ordered as it hovered over Ferra's midsection. Molly placed one hand on the Artican's chest and the other on her upper thigh and slowly applied pressure, greatly limiting Ferra's ability to move. As soon as she was quiet, a wide purple beam radiated from Silica's lower surface. The light enveloped Ferra's abdomen and wrapped around her lower back.

Instantly the pain stopped and she let out a sigh of relief. Molly loosened her grip on Ferra since her thrashings had ceased, but she stayed in contact, gently patting Ferra's thigh. Ferra looked up at the clockwork face and smiled. In a deep voice she slurred, "I'm sorry I panicked when I woke up. I didn't notice how beautiful you were until it was too late." Ferra reached one hand up to touch the brass cheek before she passed out.

Molly looked over at Silica. "Was she flirting?" she asked, panicked. "That spring is only half wound; I'm not sure!"

The gem said nothing as she continued to heal the unconscious warrior.

CHAPTER TEN

"If there is a power greater than true love

I've yet to find it. Nor do I want to."

Lord Charmant

THE moment I saw Hawk, everything changed.

His smile, the way I knew his heart jumped the same way mine did, the knowledge that he was alive because I didn't want to live without him. In one look there was so much communicated that there were literally no words to express how I felt.

Especially when I realized… no, that's not right… especially when I *knew* he felt the same way.

Just the thought that someone somewhere might feel the same way about you as you do about them can make your whole day better. But the fact, the absolute knowledge, changes your life. I've heard this before; hell, I'd seen it every single time I watched a PG-13 movie. You always want to believe in true love, but common sense tells you the reality of it is most like a crap shoot. I had two genetic defects that were working against me, though.

The first was my dad. He swore by love at first sight since he'd only known my mom for a week before they were married. He would constantly go on about how he knew the moment his eyes met hers that they were already together; everything else was just a formality. I grew up not only believing in love at first sight but constantly reminded that I was alive and kicking because of it.

The second was that I am a gay teenage male, which means love at first sight is a lot like crystal meth to a drug addict. Disney movies were comparable to mainlining heroin, and *The Princess Diaries* and *The Cutting Edge* were just rocks to melt down for injection. No matter how much life and people told me to keep my wits about me and to take things slow, my inner romantic made me want to believe so hard it hurt.

Yet even with all of this, I had a virtual Jewel sitting on my shoulder whispering in my ear, "Do not lose your shit over the pretty boy." I was pretty much ignoring Virtual Jewel when Hawk began to complain.

"Why are the beds so damned big?" he shouted down to me, venting his frustration.

I shrugged at him as I scanned the room for something soft enough for him to land on. "Maybe Ruber's people have some huge house guests?" I remarked, noticing the rest of the furniture in the room was just as oversized. "I swear, I feel like I'm in the middle of an episode of *Batman*."

I was shocked to hear Hawk laugh.

"Who would use a giant-sized typewriter anyways?" he asked himself out loud.

I turned back and looked at him. "You know what I meant?"

He froze in midlaugh as he realized what he had just done as well. "I did," he answered, shocked. "How do I know what a typewriter is? How in the nine worlds do I know what a *Batman* is?"

"Same way I know that because of where we are, you can't use your Light charm to float off the bed," I said. I wasn't sure where the information was coming from; no, that's not all of it. The information didn't seem to be *coming* from anywhere. The only way I can explain it is that it felt like I'd learned it from my tutor when Hawk/I had been young. Just like I knew that because we had descended to a different physical plane, Hawk's magics had been altered. Our eyes met. I hadn't been trained in Royal Etiquette, so I didn't feel I needed to be polite. "What's going on?"

I could sense he knew but was somehow veiling his thoughts so I couldn't hear them. "I'm not quite sure."

I also knew that was a lie.

"I'll use these cushions," he said, grabbing the pillows behind him and tossing them down to the floor.

There was a flash of annoyance as I realized he had gotten the idea from me. "That won't work," I told him, trying to keep my thoughts to myself. "It's too far down and the pillows…."

Without a moment's hesitation, he jumped off the bed and landed perfectly in the center of a pillow. His knees bent at just the right moment to provide some shock absorption—and to make him look like a gymnast dismounting instead of a crazy man jumping off a giant bed.

Simultaneously, both of my knees exploded in pain.

The misery was so sudden and complete that my body reacted before I knew what had happened. I went down like I'd been hit by a truck. I only knew Hawk had knelt beside me when he looked into my eyes and then back at my legs and asked, "Are you okay?"

I could feel the echo of my pain through his thoughts, which were coated with his confusion as to why I was experiencing pain at all.

"Was that you?" I asked, this time the answer popping into my head the moment I asked it. The pain was what he had felt when he jumped off the bed, which shocked the living hell out of me. "It hurt *that* much?" I had to ask, since he hadn't expressed one iota of discomfort from the impact.

"I am trained to endure pain," he admitted, almost embarrassed. "Is it that bad?"

It was, but I refused to look like a total wimp in front of him. I shook my head as I forced myself not to rub my knees. "It'll pass."

His sigh told me that it wouldn't any time soon.

"We're... like, joined now, aren't we?" I asked, knowing the answer but not the depth of the linking. He knew a lot more about whatever it was than I did, but he was keeping some kind of mental firewall up. That meant the only thing I knew was that he knew *more* and wasn't telling me because of something else that he knew that I didn't. All in all, my frustration levels would have powered a small city. "Why are you keeping stuff from me?" I was getting angry and, mental link or not, there was no way he could miss that.

"Because I'm not sure what is going on." Which was a half lie. I couldn't see the other half of the lie. There was something, a word just on the edge of his mind that I couldn't quite read. Of course, the moment I knew there was something he was hiding from me was the moment I tried to figure out what it was. He felt me rummaging around in his thoughts and reacted to it. "Stop it," he snapped. "If I don't want to share something, then don't pry!"

He'd done the mental equivalent of a slap to the nose of a disobedient puppy; all that did was piss me off even more. "You want me not to pry?" I said, shoving his hands away from me. "Fine, but if you end up almost dying again, don't expect me to save you."

Even through my anger I could feel the insincerity of that statement. He smiled slightly, which just made me all the angrier. I surprised myself with my next words, because I meant them, and he knew it as soon as I did.

"I jumped through two dimensional portals so far to save you; don't count on a third." I forced myself not to hobble when I stalked away from him, and I refused to think that I had no idea where I was going.

"Okay," he called from behind me. "We are bonded." I looked over my shoulder and, when I saw that he had plopped down on the giant bed pillow, turned. He patted next to him, his way of asking me to sit down and listen. I returned to him and sat, not because he wanted me to but because my knees were still freaking killing me and standing hurt like hell.

"Go on," I prompted him. I could tell he wanted to smile at my anger, but he knew better, so just the edges of his mouth twitched.

"My people call it The Calling. It is when two people meet and have an instant connection. It's more than just physical looks and fondness, but a bond that makes them feel as if they have known each other forever." I could feel his unwillingness to believe what he was explaining. He wasn't talking about an actual thing to him; he was describing a fairy tale he had heard but never believed. Yet here I was reading his thoughts, so it made not believing that much harder. It sounded a lot like love at first sight, but I could tell there was much more involved than just that concept.

"Tell me about it," he muttered under his breath in response to my thoughts.

"But that's not the whole story, is it?" I asked carefully, knowing we were approaching the part of the subject he had been trying to hide. "There is something else you're not telling me, right?"

He nodded his head slightly. "Something impossible."

I'm not sure who was more surprised to hear me burst out laughing, him or me. "I am traveling with an ice barbarian, a talking gem, and a fairy prince I have some kind of telepathic bond with, and *now* you want to say something is impossible? I am seriously understanding why Alice needed to start the day with at least six impossible things. The impossible made the rest of all this nonsense easier to believe."

I could feel him start to ask about Alice and then get the information from my thoughts. In a matter of seconds, he knew everything I had seen or read about *Alice in Wonderland*, if not in detail, at least the generalities. In the same way, I could feel his mind recognizing the similarities between the book and movies and the realm of Aponiviso. The name Aponiviso brought with it the impression of chaos, a world that had no rules whatsoever.

"When I say impossible, I mean the word impossible," he said after we both absorbed the information from each other's minds. "Not improbable, not a long shot, but a flat-out action that is physically impossible." His words sounded angry, but I knew he was just frustrated. He was worried about his parents, the situation he was in, and me for some reason, and everything seemed to be coming to a head. "It doesn't make sense!"

There was not an ounce of weakness in his voice, but I could sense that he was on the verge of tears.

Without saying a word, I reached over and pulled him into a hug. We sat there for a while and held each other, drawing strength from where there had been none. It's kind of a private thing… so do you mind checking in on someone else?

Thanks.

RUBER knew he'd find his sister in the library. He found her double-checking that the stacks of memory stones had not been disturbed in any way from the unexpected teleportation. Though he had been away for only a few millennia, he could swear he could see differences in her. "Everything is as it should be?" he asked, floating next to her.

"You have to ask that?" she replied curtly. "You abandon your family, take off, leaving *me* to do your duties, just to turn around and bring back humans? If you were going to be gone for such a short time, why even mention it?" She teleported a stack of the book-shaped gems to another shelf. "But then again, it's always about what Raatnaraj wants."

"Are you done?" he asked before she could start talking again. "I was asking about the information, but obviously you weren't. I would suggest that, if you wish to elaborate on the fiction you're creating, you record it on an appropriate medium. I'm certain that future generations will marvel at your masterful storytelling abilities."

She turned toward him. "Your family needed you," she said, emotion creeping around the edges of her voice.

"My *family* sent me away," he countered, his voice as firm as always. "Father never has and never will accept my choice when I decided my life path. You have to know that."

"You didn't even try to convince him otherwise!" Caerus's voice grew louder.

"We argued about it for over two thousand years, Caerus."

"*See*?" she practically shouted. "We've spent more time arguing over bedroom selections! Two thousand years is almost nothing."

"Caerus," he said in a much warmer tone. "I wanted to do something different with my life. That is not going to change. Father wanted me to do something else, and that is not going to change. How much longer would you have had us debate?"

"But you just left." Her voice was barely a whisper.

"I was sent away, given as a gift to the royal family of Arcadia on behalf of the Crystal Court." He forced his voice to remain dispassionate as he explained to his sister what had happened. "Father said if I wanted to learn about others so much, then I could do it somewhere else."

"You could have fought it," Caerus argued halfheartedly.

"I could have, but I wanted to be free to do the things I wanted to do, and I couldn't do them staying here. What was the alternative?"

Before she could answer, the doors to the library opened. A squad of amber guards remained just outside the door in formation. A green amber senior officer floated straight into the room, turned itself at a ninety-degree angle, and stopped in front of Ruber. "Your father is ready to see you and your… visitors." The way the amber paused before saying the word "visitors" told Ruber more than the tone of the fossilized resin's voice. "You are to collect them and follow us to the throne room."

"This bodes well," Ruber muttered quietly as he floated out of the room and assumed his position next to the ambers.

ADAMAS had ruled the Crystal Court as long as anyone could remember.

With the exception of some of the very long-lived dwarves of Kh'zdule and the Construct of Justice, there was no one left alive in Djupur Byrjun who could remember a time before Adamas's reign. When he rose up against the rule of Pyrite and seized control of the court all those years ago, he changed the way the gem elementals interacted with the rest of the realm for all of time. Reversing Pyrite's policy of involvement in politics, Adamas reforged the court into a repository of knowledge that had successfully maintained its neutrality for millennia. Only after Titania Ascended, making Faerth the center of the realms, and the ever-shrinking supply of natural resources had pushed the Gnome King and the Dwarves into combat, had the Court been pushed into action.

However slow that action might be.

No one rushed Adamas into making a decision, no one at all. When he had been told his wayward son had appeared in the library with a collection of humans in tow, his first thought had been that either the Dwarves or the Gnome King were attempting to force his decision. However, once Caerus had reported that their surprise arrival actually was of Raatnaraj's doing, and that he looked as if he'd been in a conflict, Adamas decided there was no ruse.

That was when he summoned his "guests."

Moments later his son floated in, accompanied by two dark elves and two pale beings he assumed were fairies.

Unlike most of his kin, Adamas was more attuned to the passage of time as it occurred with mortal beings and was conscious of how long Ruber had been gone. A majority of the other gem elementals measured time in a geological sense, which meant, to them, thousands of years weren't even noticeable. Adamas's father, who had been a diamond himself, could remember the time before even Dwarves walked the lands. Adamas's father had given up his energies and returned to his inert form, having been sentient for over two million years. Since he'd been inert for 2.1 billion years before that, his life was viewed as regrettably brief. In comparison to those vast numbers, Ruber's absence could have been him walking out of the room.

Adamas had noticed.

"Father," Ruber said, taking a moment to descend sharply and rise again equally swiftly, the gem equivalent of a formal bow. "You look well."

"I am indestructible," the shield-cut diamond responded, negating the compliment entirely. "You're back." The two words were in no way a question, nor even a statement. They were a declaration of dissatisfaction to anyone within earshot.

"There were circumstances beyond my control," Ruber answered in a precise reflection of his father's cold tone of voice. "I had no choice."

"You always have a choice." Adamas sniffed, floating past Ruber to examine the pale beings more closely. He paused at Hawk and Kane, giving them both a gem's equivalent of a hard stare. "Are you brothers?" he asked them after a few seconds.

Kane started to cough in shock as Hawk patted his back and answered. "No, sire, we are not."

"Odd," he said distantly, floating toward the dark elves.

"Odd why?" Hawk asked, his voice tinged with anger.

Adamas ignored his question as he examined Ater. "You are a royal assassin, correct?"

"I was," Ater answered, his voice as respectful as if he were speaking to Titania herself.

"You *were* as in you are no longer an assassin?" the diamond asked.

"I *was* as in I no longer work for the royal family."

"But still a killer," the king said, floating away from the pair, dismissing them both instantly. "So which one of you is the heir?" he asked, floating back to the stone pillar he used as a throne.

Hawk looked at Ruber, confused, before answering. "I am, your lordship." In a whisper, he asked the ruby, "He can't detect the only fairy in the room?"

Before Ruber could answer, Adamas interrupted in a louder voice, "If there were a full-blooded fairy in the room, I could indeed detect it. I am asking, however, which of the two mongrels present has royal blood flowing through his veins?"

Kane grabbed Hawk as he began to charge the diamond. "Mongrel?" he roared. "You dare to insult the heir to the throne of Arcadia?"

"Ah, so it is you," Adamas said, sounding bored with the entire conversation. "I take it, from the manner of your appearance in my realm, that this is not a state visit."

"Hawk, slow your roll," Kane whispered in his ear when the prince didn't stop trying to free himself and go after the diamond.

"Yes, Hawk, whatever your *roll* is, I'd advise you to slow it," Adamas echoed. A flash of light appeared inside the King's core. Seconds later, the humans were surrounded by two dozen ambers, all of them glowing with magical energies. "Your friends have abysmal manners," he said to Ruber.

"Yes, of course, it is they are the ones lacking in manners," Ruber snapped, floating closer to his father. "Not the pompous head of state who goads and provokes his guests for no other reason than to display his power over them."

"Guests?" Adamas asked and then paused to look at his son. "The term 'guests' would imply that they are welcome here."

"I welcomed them here," Ruber said, a glow beginning to form in his core.

"And that would assume you are welcome here."

No one breathed, much less spoke, as the two gems glared at each other.

"Silica," Ruber called out, knowing the nurse amethyst would be close by to give a report about the last member of their party. "How much time does the Frigus need before she can be moved?"

The huge purple gem floated out of the shadows. "If she remains still, I would estimate she would be ready within six hours. The clockwork girl seems to be keeping her calm."

"On behalf of the Arcadian royal family, I beseech you for six hours of sanctuary," Ruber said with all the formality of a diplomat. "After that, we will be on our way."

"You can speak on behalf of the Arcadian throne now?" Adamas asked, sarcasm lacing his words.

"No, but the mongrel can," Hawk snarled. He glanced quickly at Kane and nodded encouragingly. Reluctant still, Kane loosened his grasp. Taking two paces toward the King, Hawk stated, "I am Hawk'keen Maragold, Prince of Arcadia and heir to the throne. One day I shall rule the Center of the Realms and they will answer to my command."

"I'm happy for you," Adamas commented acidly.

"You should be," Hawk said, taking another step closer to the arrogant diamond. "You should be ecstatic for my future Ascension. Do you know why?"

The gem sounded bored. "Why?"

Hawk's eyes narrowed as he growled, "Because I won't forget this."

After several pregnant seconds, Adamas said to the ambers, "Show my son and his guests to their rooms. Make sure their needs are attended to."

The amber gems led the procession out of the throne room, Hawk glaring at the diamond the entire time. "Ruber, a moment," the gem lord asked.

When Kane paused at the door, the ruby told him, "It's all right. I will catch up." Reluctantly the human followed Hawk from the chamber, leaving father and son alone.

"This is why you left?" Adamas asked, his irritation and cynicism overflowing. "So you could wander around with killers and half-breeds?"

"They are my friends!" Ruber shouted, the light inside him flaring in concert with his words. "Besides, what concern is it of yours?" he added, gathering his composure. "You were the one who 'gave' me to the Arcadians in the first place."

Adamas seemed unfazed by the accusation. "You wanted to travel; I gave you the opportunity."

"Don't you dare," Ruber threatened. "Do not attempt to make it sound like you did anything for my own well-being. I refused to live the life you wanted for me, so you sold me like I was property."

"I gave you life," the king responded, the first warnings of anger creeping into his voice. "You literally exist because I willed you to do so! Your life is mine to control. That is our way."

Ruber got as close as he could to his father without physically touching him. "And you hated your father for his control over you from the time of your creation, Father, until the minute he relinquished his sentience. Don't think I don't know that. Six hours, Father, and then I am out of your life. I would like to think we can get through such an insignificant amount of time without further conversation."

Not waiting to be dismissed, Ruber turned and floated out of the room, suddenly remembering every reason he had left this place the first time.

AS SOON as we were alone, I turned to Hawk. "Clockwork girl?" He shrugged, pretty much verifying that neither one of us knew what the hell was going on. "So we can all agree that Ruber's dad is a dick?"

Hawk chuckled at my joke. The two elves, however, stared at me, their expressions puzzled. I wasn't sure if Hawk's mind was reinforcing my own or if I was suffering from a complete lack of a shit to give, but instead of shrinking away from the stares, I glared back at them and asked, "Are you trying to be rude, or is everyone allowed to stare at me like I'm a talking dog?"

Hawk looked over at me and then to them, confusion on his face also. "What is the problem?" he asked the first one.

Distantly I knew his name was Ater.

Ater looked from me to Hawk and then back to me. "How is he speaking our language?" he asked Hawk, talking as if I wasn't in the room. "I was under the impression that the ruby was providing translation."

Holy shit, I was speaking fairy? I thought to myself.

"Holy shit, I'm speaking fairy!" I said out loud.

"I cast a Babel spell," Hawk lied with an ease that was unnerving. "Depending on the gemstone is a tactical liability."

Hawk had said exactly what the two wary, suspicious dark elves needed to hear. I kept quiet while Hawk cautioned me not to contradict him aloud. I had already guessed that the two dark elves were incredibly dangerous. Hawk showed me some memories that more than told me I was right. I decided that shutting up was the best idea I'd heard in several days. I could understand why he didn't want anyone knowing about the Calling—or at least I thought I could understand. His thoughts about us were shielded, and I didn't get why.

"I wasn't aware you were that skilled in The Arts," Ater commented as he began to examine the room in detail, looking for any hidden compartments or places where a person could eavesdrop. The other one, Pullus, did the same on the far side of the chamber. He said nothing at all, letting his partner speak for them. "We have a problem," he added once he was sure we were as unobserved as possible.

"Besides the fact you tried to kill me?" Hawk asked, curiosity overriding any anger he might have felt.

Ater considered Hawk's question briefly and then amended himself. "We have two problems." When it was obvious Hawk wasn't going to contradict him, he went on. "The Dark was attacking the capital when we left."

I could feel Hawk's panic move through him like ice water even though his expression remained calm and his body didn't flinch or shift position. "My family?" he asked, forcing his voice to be neutral. I ached to move closer to him and take his hand, but I knew he would be furious because, in his mind, letting me comfort him would be a sign of weakness.

I mentally told him what I thought of his macho bullshit.

"I fear they have been betrayed by Puck," Ater admitted, showing no remorse at all, simply relaying the facts as he knew them.

The name "Puck" clicked in Hawk's mind and triggered a stream of memories that was rapidly sorted as he searched for a common denominator for all of them. Although his mind moved much too quickly for me to keep up, one name recurred again and again, a name I knew well.

"Spike?" I asked him as he struggled to bottle up the disbelief and fury that threatened to explode into visible rage.

Hawk nodded. "Puck is Spike's sire. This all begins to make sense."

I couldn't believe the calmness in Hawk's tone. From the look on Pullus's face, neither could he. I cocked my head to one side and wondered about the quiet dark elf.

"Spike was the one who sent us to learn the secret of Ascension," the First explained to Hawk. "He made it quite clear that you were not to come back with it."

I watched Hawk stare at the ground for almost a minute without saying a word. I wasn't even sure he was still breathing. The only way I knew he was actually doing something was the dark cloud that had become his thoughts. Ater stood silently, waiting for the prince's next words.

"You betrayed the throne," Hawk stated after what seemed like an hour and a half of uncomfortable silence.

Ater nodded and, in a move that would have been the envy of any magician, made a knife appear in his hand. I lurched to get between him and Hawk, but the dark elf turned the blade around and offered the hilt to Hawk as he went down to one knee. "Our lives are yours to take," he said, looking down to the ground, baring the back of his neck. Pullus knelt beside Ater, silent as ever.

I could feel the desire to kill Ater in Hawk's mind, so strongly that I was half certain *I* wanted to kill him myself. I held my breath as I waited for Hawk to take the knife and kill Ater and Pullus with one slice.

"I'll kill you later," Hawk said, ignoring the blade altogether. "Right now you still serve the throne and for the time being, I *am* the throne." He looked down, locking eyes with Ater. "Do you understand me?"

Ater nodded once, his expression completely unreadable to me. Pullus echoed the motion, although I wondered if Hawk had seen it. Between us, he thought, "I did."

"We need to know if the capital has fallen or not," Hawk said aloud, turning away, purposely exposing his back to the dark elf.

Before anyone could say anything more, a bright green stone with a British child's voice popped out of the bedding and exclaimed, "It has! The Arcadian capital has already fallen!!" When we all stared at him, I could imagine Lates taking a large gulp before saying, "Oh, right. Hullo there, I'm Rat… er, Ruber's brother."

I could see Ater look to Hawk and silently ask him for permission to kill the talking rock. Thank God Ruber came in before Hawk had to answer.

CHAPTER ELEVEN

"There are no secrets in the Nine Realms.
There are only things that we do not talk about."
Molly Luna Gato
Former resident of The Farm

THE concept of pandimensionality is a complicated one to grasp.

In a nutshell, it means there are parts of planes of existence that intersect parts of every other plane in one way or another. For example, the winds that are created in Aponiviso, the realm of sky and air, move through the atmosphere of every world where people breathe oxygen. Certain beings like genies or sylphid can move from one plane to another by finding thin spots between two worlds and using the air as the medium for facilitation. It is this phenomenon that causes certain words to be carried much farther than they would on their own as part of normal speech. They access the intersection points and travel along them.

Djupur Byrjun works on the same concept, except the medium is the earth instead of air.

The Crystal Court had mastered the ability to move from realm to realm using the earth as its facilitating medium. This capability had given them access to one of the most valuable resources in their world: information. Adamas's agents traveled unnoticed through the nine realms, everywhere gathering information about the inhabitants, recording every event that occurred between them, learning everything.

These agents were called back to the court on a regular basis. The knowledge each had acquired was recorded and preserved in enchanted stones, designed to be vast storage devices for the accumulated knowledge of the Crystal Court. With the exception of the Lost Book of Potmos, which was owned by Inmediares, the southern witch of Aus, the Court's collection of information was the greatest in the Nine Realms.

All of this was, of course, known to Ruber. What he had not known was that his younger brother had been using his powers to spy on distant events without his father's permission.

"Are you insane?" Ruber exclaimed, slamming the door shut behind him.

The other humans in the room could not see the dimensional energies bleeding off the younger gem, so they had no idea he had not just appeared from under the bedclothes but from under the ground beneath the bed.

"What?" Lates answered automatically, in the tone all teenage boys have used since the dawn of time when confronted with the fact they had been caught.

Deny, deny, deny.

"I wasn't doing anything!" Lates lied, floating away from Ruber.

"Are you trying to get yourself killed?" Ruber pressed, his voice rising in anger. "Do you know what's out there?"

"I can take care of myself," the emerald insisted, dropping any pretense that he hadn't been moving through different worlds.

A pulse of energy shot out from Ruber and hit Lates dead on, dropping him out of the air instantly. The younger gem cried out in pain as his brother floated down nearer to him. "No you can't. On a scale from one to ten, that was a four in the magical Arts. Now would you like to answer again?"

Before Lates could respond, Kane stepped between the two gems. "Ruber! Back off! He's hurt." He picked up the smaller emerald. "Are you okay?"

For a moment it looked as if Lates was going to accept the human's kindness, but out of nowhere he exploded in anger, hurtling away from Kane. "I am not a baby!" He darted toward the door, pausing and saying to Ruber, "You're worse than Father!" Before his brother could respond, Lates passed through the stone wall as if it were water and fled the room.

"What did he mean that the capital has already fallen?" Hawk asked after a few seconds of silence.

Ruber said nothing, too distracted by Lates's dangerous actions and accusation to reply.

"Ruber!" Hawk barked. "What was he talking about?"

Kane was hesitant to touch his friend. Instead, he asked him quietly, "Ruber, what's wrong?"

"He was right," the ruby said, sounding completely depressed. "I did sound exactly like my father."

Hawk took a few steps closer to the gem. "By all that is holy, Ruber, what did he mean by 'the capital has fallen'?"

"I have no idea," the gem admitted, trying to shrug off the melancholy mood that had descended on him. "I have no more information than you. I have been denied access to my family's accumulation of knowledge. But I do know someone who will help." He floated away from Kane and Hawk. "Give me a few seconds to find my sister."

He passed through the stone wall as well.

Kane looked over at Hawk. "I'm a little foggy on how you make a living rock. I mean, is there a mommy rock and a daddy rock and they get together and listen to some Barry White?"

Ater looked at Pullus and then over to Hawk. "I understood everything he said, but it made no sense. Is the enchantment degrading?"

Hawk shook his head and said to the dark elves, "I don't know who Barry White is either," and then to Kane, "nor am I conversant in the sexual reproduction habits of gem elementals." He sighed angrily and sat down on a chair carved out of stone. "And I don't care."

Kane walked over to him and pulled him into a hug.

"I'm afraid my mom is dead," Hawk whispered to him as he leaned into Kane.

Kane just nodded and held him close, because he honestly had no idea what to say.

FERRA woke up to an argument being held entirely in whispers.

"She isn't ready to be moved yet!"

Even in a whisper, the clockwork girl's brassy tone could be identified.

"What she is ready for or not is irrelevant at this point," another female voice argued. The warrior had retained a vague memory of a purple gem, one of Ruber's people no doubt, but the salient facts were lost in the haze of pain that permeated Ferra's current state. "Adamas has ruled that she and the other humans are to be gone within the day, which means in six hours she is going to have to leave no matter what her condition."

"I thought you were supposed to be a healer," Molly's voice admonished the amethyst.

The offense in the gem's voice was obvious as she shot back, "I am Silica Appolonia Medens, and my life purpose is to understand how human bodies work. I will do my best to keep the blue woman alive, but her well-being does not and will never rank above my loyalty to the Crystal Court."

"Then don't ever call yourself a doctor," Molly hissed, the faint sound of a steam whistle mixing with her words.

"I never would," the gem said, her voice fading as she floated away.

Ferra felt a damp towel on her forehead as Molly mumbled to herself. "Going to wait for my Etiquette spring to wind down and then tell that horrid gem how I really feel." She stopped when she saw her patient was staring up at her. "Oh, you're awake!" she exclaimed happily. "Are you in pain? Discomfort? Because if you are, I can force that floating purple blower to come back and make you feel better."

"Blower?" Ferra asked, smiling unconsciously at the brass face that was trying to express frustration without much success. The two metal irises around her eyes had half closed in an attempt to look like they were narrowed in anger, but that honestly made her look like she was tired. "I don't understand that word."

"It's the harshest word I can use with my etiquette spring this tightly wound. Give me an hour or two and my words will start becoming more commonplace."

Even half dazed from her injuries, Ferra had to break out in laughter at the brass girl's obvious frustration. She was just plain adorable. "You're funny," she said out loud.

Molly looked back down at her. "Oh, are we flirting again? My Coquette spring is wound tightly now, so I am far more prepared than I was."

The barbarian froze in her bed at Molly's words.

Unaware of Ferra's reaction, the clockwork girl continued, "I have to admit, even with it completely set, I find most forms of flirting confusing. There is such a fine line between being forthcoming and being a toffer that I sometimes get confused."

"I was not flirting," Ferra informed her, her voice as cold as the winds of her homeland.

Molly paused; the sound of whirring gears inside her head was audible as she thought. "Oh," she replied after a few seconds. "Because when you said, '*I didn't notice how beautiful you were until it was too late*,' I assumed you were flirting."

Ferra was doubly shocked. First, Molly had quoted her words in Ferra's own voice, played back after being recorded on an ancient metal data cylinder, and second, because Ferra had never expressed such feelings out loud before. "I didn't say that!" Ferra practically roared, trying to sit up. "To express such ideas would be a sin against Logos."

This time Molly was having none of Ferra's attempts at movement.

She pushed the larger woman back into the bed with one metal hand, exerting no effort whatsoever to keep her in place. "You can't move again. The magic that is healing you needs time to work." Her voice was still cheery, but Ferra could detect a harshness that had entered it, as if the clockwork girl were becoming upset. "And you *did* say that. I am incapable of lying, so to imply that I did is a great insult." Ferra opened her mouth to protest, but Molly talked over her. "Now, if you have some form of cultural taboo that prevents you from admitting your feelings to another, then I apologize. I haven't been serviced in centuries, and my information about other lands might be outdated. But I refuse to allow you to further harm yourself because you're upset that I violated a tradition. Instead of talking, why don't we just sit here and wait for you to heal."

It was a statement, not a question.

After about a minute, Ferra attempted to ask, "Can you move your hand?" but never got past the "you" before Molly interrupted her. "*No* talking."

Ferra sighed and settled back down, willing herself to heal faster.

RUBER found Caerus in the library again; this time she had a large book-sized opal sitting on the table. An image of an iridescent gem was projected above it, and floating next to it were images of Ruber and Caerus, though much smaller than they were now.

"Is that Mother?" he asked, floating out of the shadows toward her.

The sapphire looked startled, banishing the image with a flash of energy. "I didn't see you there!" she exclaimed.

"I wasn't aware that Mother had recorded her memories," Ruber said, floating nearer the book. "When was this done?"

Caerus looked as if she were going to continue to argue but, after a sigh, she admitted, "I found them under a series of recordings about

Father's coronation. I think Beryl donated them."

"Beryl!" Ruber said, amazement in his voice. "I had forgotten about him!" He laughed, and after a few seconds his sister joined him. "Do you remember the time he tried to teach us how to master dimensional portals, and we summoned that flock of volo haplorhines?" Caerus's laughter was like the sound of crystal pieces tinkling together when a chandelier is disturbed by a passing breeze.

"I still think there are some on the surface," she said, still laughing. "I remember Father screaming through the halls that there was monkey crap on his throne."

Ruber tried to talk though his own laughing. "Truth be told? That was me, not the monkeys."

"*Ruber!*" she cried out in shock. "You didn't!"

"I did," he admitted, attempting to stifle another laugh and failing miserably. "Who do you think ported them out when Father declared an open hunting season against them? I couldn't stand the thought of them dying for my actions."

"You could have just admitted you were the guilty party," she brought up, laughter spluttering around her words.

"Are you insane? Then he would have come after *me*!"

They both broke out laughing again.

"Why did you leave, Ruber?" she asked in a softer voice. "One year you were here and the next you were gone."

"Father gave me an ultimatum," Ruber replied soberly. "I decided to call him on it."

"Why not just stay and learn how to rule?" she asked. "How bad could it have been?"

Ruber flew upward in anger. "I didn't want to do it!" he proclaimed loudly. "Why do we have no control over our own destiny? Why aren't our lives our own?"

"You know how it is," Caerus answered him. "Our sires give us their energies, so our existence is literally theirs to control."

"Only because they say so!" Ruber raged. "Life forms all over the realms allow their young to live their own lives. Why not us?"

The pink stone flared in response as she floated up toward him. "They also kill each other over gold and land. Should we emulate that as well?"

"Smoke and mirrors, Caerus, that's smoke and mirrors. I didn't want to do this," Ruber said, trying to keep his voice level. "I didn't want to have this fight again."

"Then admit you were wrong," she pressed him.

"Wrong?" he shouted back. "What about you, Caerus? Do you wish to spend your life just trying to look perfect and obtainable? Is that your life goal?"

"It is what Father wants," she answered wearily.

"But what do *you* want?" he asked.

She didn't say anything for a long while before answering quietly, "It's what I was made to do."

"Rubbish!" he cried, frustration echoing through his words. "You *want* to do *this*! You want to be a historian." He flew down to the stacks of memory stones. "This is how you want to live your life, this has always been. You love being down here, examining the records. It is your passion and we both know it. Have you ever tried to tell Father?"

"Tell him what?" she practically screamed back. "Tell him that I want to be more than just a pretty facet? That the only time I feel alive is when I am going over our memories and discovering where we come from? What good would that do, Raatnaraj?" Her voice became calmer, and she floated back toward the books. "Our life is laid out before us, and it is not our place to argue against it."

"Our place? Our *place*?" Ruber exclaimed, following her down. "And what was Father's *place* under Pyrite? Did he just sit back and accept it? No! He didn't!" Very gently, he asked, "Why should it be any different for us?"

In a voice barely above a whisper, she said, "I don't know; it just is."

The two of them floated there in silence for several minutes, neither one knowing what to say next. Finally Ruber spoke. "Caerus, I need the most current intelligence we have for Arcadia, most specifically for the royal family." Before she could argue with him, he stressed to her, "That boy in the next room is the heir to the throne. If that isn't enough, I am fairly certain he is hiding the secret of Ascension on him, so when I say the more we can do to further his endeavors the better off the Crystal Court will be, I do so with good cause."

She considered his words carefully before zipping away from him and toward another stack of stones. "We haven't kept someone stationed around Arcadia because of the djinn."

Ruber froze. "Djinn?"

She kept moving the books out of the way, looking for one in particular. "The last agent we had there was Citrina. She reported the changeling had managed to get its claws on a bound djinn. Given the situation in Arcadia, it was only a matter of time before it was let loose. Since there really is no way for our kind to defend against that kind of power, she was recalled." Silence followed her statement, but Caerus didn't notice: she had located the tablet she wanted and levitated it to pass it to her brother. "Ruber, did you still want the reports…," she began to ask but stopped when she noticed Ruber had already left the library. He was flying as fast as he could back to the room where he had left the others.

He was going to be too late.

LOOKING at the world through Hawk's eyes was weird.

No, I didn't say that right. I wasn't seeing the world just through Hawk's eyes; I was looking at and also remembering it through Hawk's mind. Uhm… maybe if I give you an example. Take the two dark elves. Now, just from my own experiences, they scared the hell out of me. I mean, I saw these guys in action, and I know how insanely deadly they could be. I know the one who actually stabbed Hawk in the neck is dead, but when I look at those two, I can't get rid of the memory that they had the same to-do list as the dead one. Then Hawk's memories come storming in, and I have to deal with them as well.

I already knew their names—Ater and Pullus—and that they were two of a trio of dark elf assassins who had worked for the Throne since before Hawk was born. The more I thought about them, the more I/Hawk remembered. Like the fact that one of the trio had been killed about a year before Ater, Pullus, and the now-dead elf showed up in my world, and that the one guy I saw die at Jewel's was his replacement. I also "remembered" that Ater and Pullus were a bonded pair, which seemed to be a mixture of brothers, partners, and lovers that only made sense if you were a dark elf. I could also sense Hawk's displeasure that the two of them had switched sides to work for Puck so easily.

"I am not fond of finding out the gems have spies in our land," Ater commented.

Hawk's anger spiked at the words "our land," but I could feel him clamp down on the emotion and the desire to remind the dark elf that, after his and Pullus's actions, Arcadia wasn't exactly their land anymore.

"I am more concerned about the capital," Hawk replied without looking up.

Mentally, he had thought "my mother" rather than "the capital," but the sentiment was basically the same. "If Puck has taken control of the palace, that might mean he controls the palace's enchantments. That would make taking it back that much more difficult."

I saw Ater look at Pullus and realized that some kind of unspoken conversation was taking place between them. Finally, the First looked at Hawk. "You can't be thinking of trying to confront the changeling."

Hawk looked up and gave him a dark stare. "Are you really trying to dictate what I am thinking?" What Hawk really meant was that he couldn't believe, after what they had done, that they hadn't instantly fallen at his feet to do whatever he ordered. However, he had no intention of saying that aloud.

"Even if he doesn't control the palace, he still controls the Dark," Ater explained patiently. "It would be a futile attempt."

Hawk recoiled like he had drunk spoiled milk at the mention of the Dark. Unable to look at the Elves any longer, he turned his gaze away. "I cannot believe Puck was able to deceive them enough to have them turn on my family."

Ater opened his mouth to answer when Pullus stood up and spoke instead. "He didn't deceive anyone."

I was as shocked as Hawk was: those four words were the most I'd heard from the Second since we'd met back up. I also knew that when Ater was present, their protocol was for him to speak for the two of them. For Pullus to break protocol was akin to him dropping an f-bomb. "Excuse me?" Hawk asked, icicles practically dripping off his words.

"They weren't deceived about anything," Pullus repeated, ignoring Ater's halting touch on his arm. "Puck may have exploited their desire for equality and turned that toward violence, but the Dark has resented your family since time immemorial."

I felt Hawk's reactions tumble around from anger to outrage to guilt back to anger in a split second, his mouth half-open as he tried to formulate a response. Finally he was able to get one word out and that just barely. "Why?"

"You know why."

Oh my God, that was me.

Hawk turned and gaped at me. "What?"

I could feel his hurt and betrayal as he looked at me, but I forced myself not to give in. "You know why they resent your family, Hawk," I repeated with a little more force. "You know how they treated the Dark for… well, forever. You saw it and part of you hated it as well, but you just never did anything about it." I knew this because he knew this, and even though he tried to silence his thoughts, it was too late; I already knew what the truth was. "You talk a good game about how your people are perfect and therefore superior, but at the end of the day you know it just makes them a bunch of dicks. If your people were being treated that way, you would have declared war eons ago."

Hawk opened his mouth, and, I have to be honest, I had no idea what he was about to say.

I guess I'll never know, since at that very moment Ater asked, "Do you smell smoke?"

Which was just before all hell broke loose.

ADAMAS was sitting in the throne room, thinking, when he felt the first throbbing vibration.

Only a being soulbound to the earth could experience what the head of the Crystal Court felt then. The vibration began far below a human's ability to hear or feel, far below the range of normal detection devices. Adamas had felt this particular vibration many times in his long sentience, but not sitting outside the earth in which the vibration began.

He identified what that vibration meant a fraction of a second too late. An explosion, so great it shook the entire cavern, was all the warning Adamas had. "*Intruder*!" he shouted as he barreled out into the corridor. Something had traveled pandimensionally in the same way the gems did and had infiltrated the Court.

Ruber whipped around the corner into the quarters where Hawk, Kane, Ater, and Pullus stood. The ruby arrived just in time to watch the bed explode upward when a pillar of fire erupted under it. Whatever was attacking had used the same passage Lates had taken only a short while before. Ruber realized that his brother had been followed, but there was no time to waste in thought.

"Get out now!" Ruber shouted at them. The streaming, snapping flames began to coalesce into a form.

Within seconds, the djinn's body had solidified. Silent except for the sound of dying flame, the efreet glared savagely at his prey.

"*Run!*" Ruber yelled as he flew up to intercept the fiery creature.

The dark elves shepherded Hawk and Kane out of the room. Focusing entirely on protecting his friends, Ruber powered his energies until he looked like a miniature sun. "You are not welcome here, efreet," the ruby proclaimed when he was at its eye level. "Leave."

A bolt of pure energy hit the djinn between its eyes, staggering it.

Hawk had paused at the doorway to look back. Only Ater's reflexes saved the prince's life as he yanked him back just before Ruber came hurtling out of the room. The efreet had grabbed the ruby blindly, snagging it out of the air and throwing it at the wall as hard as it could.

Ruber hit the far wall and shattering on impact, scattering pieces of himself like shrapnel everywhere.

A piece slashed Kane's cheek, the force of the impact and the pain enough to send him to the ground. His vision shaky, he squinted and peered up at the satanic form lumbering toward him and the door beyond. His speed so great he sounded like a miniature F-15, Adamas flew over Kane's head and led the assault. Beside him, twenty ambers broke into squadrons of five each and, with Adamas's squadron taking point, charged the room. Flashes of energy hit the djinn from all sides and the battle was met.

Still dazed, Kane looked away from the fight and saw the darkened pieces of his friend scattered all over the floor. "Ruber?" he called out faintly. He managed to get to his hands and knees. Walking on his knees, body bent over so he could see clearly, he began to pick up the larger pieces and swept the smaller bits into a pile. Tears dripped unnoticed from his eyes, and all he said was, "Ruber—no. No."

"Kane, we have to *go*," Hawk urged. Never losing sight of the battle, ducking stray energy bolts, the prince attempted to pull Kane to his feet. But Kane refused to move.

"If we can get him together, maybe he can heal…." He choked, holding the bits and shards tight against his chest, looking for any more stray pieces. "If we—"

"Kane," Hawk said softly.

The human knew what the prince was going to say before he said it. A gem elemental's life force is contained within the latticework of its body the same way human bodies contained blood. Hawk knew Ruber was dead the moment he hit the far wall. The thought that there was nothing anyone could do flowed from Hawk's mind to Kane's.

"*You're wrong*!" Kane snapped, slapping Hawk's hand away as hard as he could. "He's in his home; there is power here—power to heal," he muttered, carefully forming all the pieces of Ruber that he'd been able to find into a pile of broken red rocks. "Power enough to heal him.... I won't let you down, Ruber. Power enough here...."

Hawk saw three ambers turn ash-black as the efreet destroyed them with a blast of arcane fire. "He's dead!" he repeated, grabbing Kane's arm, pulling him up against his will.

Kane turned to him and declared in a voice that was eerily without emotion. "You're wrong."

His eyes had been replaced with two orbs of glowing light.

Hawk stumbled backward as Kane knelt down again next to the pile. "He can heal, this place has power; it's where he was born. It's just a matter of keeping him together...." He placed both hands over the heap and pressed them together as hard as he could, compressing the fragments of dead ruby into the smallest pile possible.

Ater was about to ask Hawk what the human was doing when a glow sputtered to life inside of Kane's hands.

"He'll be okay, he's going to be okay," Kane repeated over and over, unaware that the corridor had filled with raw magic, responding to Kane's need, to his unspoken call. When hot magic hit the cool corridor air, a wind sprang to life, throwing dirt everywhere. And all the while, Kane knelt, hands cupped as they had been around Ruber's remains. The glow from beneath Kane's hands intensified. Shadows were thrown onto the ceiling as the pile of rocks began to glow as if they were white hot.

"What's he doing?" Ater shouted. The roar of the power became loud enough to drown out the sounds of the battle in the next room.

"I have no idea," Hawk said distantly as he watched Kane bring Ruber back from the dead.

Streams of energy flashed out from the gaps between Kane's hands. Like small bolts of lightning, they struck out everywhere, hitting the walls and ceiling while the light grew brighter and brighter still. The sound became so horrific that the elves and Hawk were forced to cover their ears. Around them, the hallway was filled with light. Abruptly, the wind dropped, and all Hawk could hear was a whine of energy. "*Don't look!*" he shouted just in time. There was a discharge of light from the rocks, a pulse so bright the prince could see the bones of his hands through his closed eyes. Minutes passed in which he could only see darkness behind his lids. Slowly he opened his eyes.

Hawk could not believe what he saw when he looked at Kane.

Kane held what looked like a weakened but obviously intact Ruber in his hands. The light from the gem was barely visible, but he was in one piece. There was no sign of his recent shattering.

Moving slowly, Kane got to his feet but could do no more. He wavered in place and looked for Hawk. The prince started toward him and Kane smiled. "Okay. Let's…," he began to say. Then his world spun crazily and he began to faint.

Hawk caught him and Ruber as they tumbled to the ground. The prince was still not sure what had just happened. And how what had just happened *had* happened.

Hawk had no time to think because, at that moment, Adamas flew out of the demolished guest quarters. He cried out a word of power and a diamond barrier began to form across the doorway. The djinn collided with it as it charged after Adamas. "This won't hold me, you bauble!" it bellowed as it began to pound at the barrier with all its might.

"He's right," the diamond said to the humans. "It won't hold. We must fall back."

No one mentioned the fact that the ambers he had flown in with were no longer with him. Hawk picked up Kane and without another word they began to flee back down the hall, away from the guest quarters.

THE explosion woke Ferra instantly.

She hadn't even realized she had dozed off until her eyes flew open when the chamber shook. She tried to get up again but Molly's hand still held her down. "You shouldn't move."

Ferra looked up at the beautifully carved face and found herself smiling despite her worry. "I would love to argue with you about this, but I believe my friends are in danger. That means they need me." She placed both hands on top of Molly's brass one. "I do not wish to harm anything as unique as you, but if you don't let me up, I will be forced to move you *to* get up. I can't ensure your safety if that happens."

Seeing there was no stopping the barbarian without further harming her, Molly allowed her hand to be moved aside, which gave the barbarian the room to stand up. "Which way to my friends?"

Molly pointed to a door across the chamber. "The guest quarters are that way."

"Thank you," Ferra said, pausing for a moment as if she were going to say something else to her. The brass girl waited anxiously. Instead Ferra turned toward the door and ran, never looking back.

"Now *that* time she was flirting," Molly said to herself, nodding. "I am fully wound, and she *was* flirting!" Once she realized she had been left alone, and curious about the possibility of more flirting, Molly followed Ferra down the corridor.

Chaos engulfed Ferra as she entered the hallway. Gems of all types flew by her, some nearly hitting her head, one zipping between her legs in its rush for the door. The Artican warrior assumed their uncertain courses were a gem's equivalent of panic. Others moved quickly and surely through the din.

She knew those were the warriors. Without hesitation, she fell in behind them.

Following them, she came across a makeshift barrier constructed out of stone at the beginning of a long hallway at a right angle to the first one. She saw Kane holding the ruby; he looked as if he were ready to collapse. Two dark elves led him and the prince practically walked over Kane's feet, he stayed so close. None of them looked like they were ready for more combat, although it was clear that they had seen some sort of action.

A floating diamond the size of her skull barked orders, sending his troops into what she assessed were good defensible positions. The suppressive fire the gems laid behind Hawk and his companions kept their enemy, whatever it was, at bay. One last scramble and elves, Faerth, human, and gem elemental cleared the barricade and dropped down behind it.

"What happened?" she asked Kane as soon as they made it behind the barrier.

He shook his head, obviously still extremely dazed. The dark elves ignored her, so she turned to Hawk for an explanation.

"Efreet attack," the fairy explained, not taking his eyes off the human. "Powerful one too." As if to accent his words, the magical barrier at the end of the hall burst apart as the fire creature slowly walked out into the hallway.

"Now," Adamas ordered quietly, and the gem army opened fire.

Bolts of energy ricocheted down the hall, forcing the creature to take cover back in the room. One of the larger ambers shouted, "Assault Team, advance!"

The other two groups of ambers laid down cover fire as the main group of soldiers made their way slowly toward the door. A gout of flame shot out of the room and, controlled by the mind that had created it, suddenly made a ninety-degree turn. In seconds the djinn's weapon had collected itself and then swept down the hallway at them. "Suppression!" the diamond ordered.

Three garnets faded out of visibility and flew directly toward the flame. They were colorless, almost invisible against the darkness of the stone walls, until the flame's hit them. They instantly changed to a bright red as the flames were drawn into them. Instead of deflecting the fire, the three garnets absorbed the energy, their color deepening to bright red as their energy levels increased. Ferra nodded when she saw the amber units use the distraction to move a few feet closer to the room. Good tactic, but expensive in terms of lost soldiers, she thought.

Which was when the djinn used its Arts to transform the air around the doorway into methane.

The three garnets exploded as the air around them ignited.

Adamas summoned a field to protect the human as the flames hurtled down the hall at them. The ambers advanced, firing bolts of energy at the efreet as they entered the room. "We need more troops!" the diamond called back as he focused energy into the field.

More gems came from around the corner, passing through the field and into combat as the efreet continued to attack. They were a blur of color to the humans, but not to Ruber or his father. In the midst of garnet streaks and amber blurs, of amethyst purples, one little green light hurtled forward. "Lates, no!" the ruler yelled as he watched his youngest son fly down the hallway.

"This is my fault!" the emerald called back. "I'll make this right!"

And he was gone into the fight.

"He can't—" Ruber said weakly from Kane's hand. "He can't survive in there." The gem attempted to levitate, but he wobbled in the air for only a few seconds before falling back into Kane's hands. "Must… get…." His glow dimmed again.

Coming out of his stupor, Kane slowly stood up and looked over at Ater. "Protect him?" he asked. One brief hesitation and then the dark elf nodded, accepting Ruber and cradling him gently.

Hawk turned Kane back to face him. "What are you planning to do?"

Kane didn't hesitate. "I'm going to help Ruber's brother."

"Against an e*freet*?" Hawk asked in shock. "Are you insane?"

"Lates is in trouble!" Kane shouted at Hawk.

"That's not our concern!" Hawk shot back. "We have to leave."

Kane pointed at Ruber. "He's family," Kane growled. "Which makes Lates family too." Far more quietly, he spoke to Ruber. "I'll bring him back, Ruber." When he turned back to Hawk, his voice shook with exhaustion, but he ignored it. "I don't care what you're going to do, but I'm going to try to help."

He took two steps toward a slightly lower part of the barrier, intent on crossing it, but Hawk stopped him.

"I can't figure out if you are the bravest person I have ever met or the most brain damaged." Their eyes met for a moment, and Kane smiled slightly, which caused Hawk to smile back. Sighing, he looked over to Ater and Pullus. "Ready to die?"

Ater looked at Pullus and then back to the prince. "Perhaps not ready, but always willing."

"Stay here," Hawk ordered Kane. He knew that the stubborn young man who had become the center of his world was bound to argue, so he spoke first. "You have no idea how to handle that thing in there," he said, and then in a lower voice, "Of course, neither do I, but at least I can fake it." More firmly, he continued, "Stay here and keep Ruber safe. I'll get Lates." He saw the doubt in Kane's eyes so he smiled reassuringly at him. "I promise."

Kane nodded and took a step back. "Come back." Ater handed Ruber back to him and, in an uncharacteristic move, patted Kane's shoulder and attempted a smile.

"Oh, I plan on it," Hawk said, laughing. He looked to the dark elves. "I have no idea what we are going to do, but let's do it as well as possible."

Pullus commented quietly behind Ater, "Outstanding plan."

"Let's move!" Hawk commanded. To the king, he added, "We'll get your son back, sire."

The diamond king opened the barrier, allowing them through. "I… I have no words." His voice trailed off when he realized how insufficient words were in a time like that.

"Save the words until we get him back," Hawk assured him. He looked back at Kane and gave him a wink before charging down the hallway ahead of Ater and Pullus. Their images became hazy as Adamas closed the field behind them.

CHAPTER TWELVE

"In real war there are no victors.
Only survivors."
Sirus Sus
Sole survivor of the Sus Family Slayings
Wolflands General History

WHEN Hawk rounded the corner into the demolished guest quarters, he forced himself not to react to what his eyes were seeing.

The ambers that had charged in before him were suspended, helpless, in midair as they were being liquefied by the auras of heat around them. Their screams made the already hellishly hot room that much more sinister. Lates was pinned between the efreet's hands as the creature tried again to crush the elemental. However, Lates's energy field would protect him, at least until it failed. From the way the field pulsed and faded, pulsed and faded, the younger gem had only seconds left before he was crushed.

Hawk summoned Truheart with a silent command and the blade appeared in his hands in a flash of blue light. The instant he gripped it, he lessened his mass and launched himself at the giant djinn, already bringing the sword down from right to left. The swing looked as if it would come down on the creature's head, so of course the djinn projected a field of protection above itself. A full three seconds passed before it realized that Hawk had adjusted his trajectory by increasing his weight and allowing the additional momentum to help drive the slashing blow he aimed just above the djinn's wrists.

Truheart flashed white when it touched the djinn's flesh.

A sound akin to a butcher's knife cutting through the meat, gristle, and bone of a ham hock marked the path of the Soul Blade as it severed the djinn's arms halfway between the wrist and the elbow. The djinn screamed in pain and a burst of burning wind exploded from the wounds, catching Hawk squarely in the chest and propelling him across the room into the far wall. He hit the stone surface hard and slid down, stunned, as the efreet held its amputated limbs up in agony, shaking them in disbelief.

The two dark elves moved as one person under the heat wave. Pullus slid across the stone floor, catching Lates before it impacted with the unforgiving surface, while Ater exploited the creature's distraction by worsening the injuries it had suffered. Bounding off the creature's right leg, he jumped over to the left leg and then back. He inched higher with each shift, so that, finally, he used the djinn's upper leg as a springboard and, one long knife held loosely in each hand, aimed for the two open wounds.

With the accuracy that only centuries of training can bring, he jammed the points of his blades to their hilts in the open wounds.

Kicking off the djinn's chest, Ater did a backflip away from it as the fire creature howled in increased agony. Ater landed in front of Pullus, who cradled the emerald to his chest, and took the moment to give his partner a half smile of congratulations that they had actually harmed the menace and survived.

Pullus never got a chance to respond as a bolt of fire hit him in the center of his back, burning away his flesh to his spine.

He died instantly, feeling no pain. Lates tumbled from Pullus's grip and rolled out into the corridor like a child's ball.

Ater watched as his lifemate hit the ground and slid to a halt, his entire back charbroiled to a blackened ash. *Pullus, wake up*, Ater thought desperately. He couldn't speak, couldn't move. *Wake up. You owe me a smile. Wake up and smile at me. I can't—wakeupwakeupwakeup.* He didn't want to touch Pullus because if he did, it would all be real. It would all be real, and he would be alone. He hadn't said he loved

Pullus, not enough times. He hadn't made love to him, not enough. And he wanted more time.

Then Hawk snapped into motion.

Coming off the wall, he moved past Ater, tossing a sharp kick to the dark elf as he pivoted into a defensive stance. Not yet in deep shock, Ater stumbled forward out of the room, tripping over Pullus's corpse as he fell to the floor in the hallway. Hawk looked back at him and narrowed his eyes for a moment.

Before the First could act, the body of his partner slid out of the room toward him. Then the door slammed shut, locking Hawk in with the djinn.

As Hawk turned around, two pillars of flame rose from the open wounds where the efreet's hands had once been. The flames grew brighter and then collapsed back into themselves. An instant later, swept by a wave of sheer power, the efreet's lower arms and hands became flesh.

The djinn flexed its fingers as it snarled at the young prince. "That," it said, indicating the door, "was a mistake."

Hawk brought Truheart up in a mocking salute. "You will deal with me and only me."

The demonic creature's mouth spread out in a leering grin. "I will deal with you the same way I dealt with your whore of a mother."

Hawk's expression didn't flicker as he returned the glare. Only the tone of his voice betrayed his fury. "Can you guess which word in that sentence has earned you a slow and painful death?"

Before the djinn could answer, Hawk launched his attack.

I SAW Ater stumble out into the hall and started getting worried. When I saw the body of Pullus follow, worried stepped up to frightened. When Hawk didn't follow the dark elves and the door slammed shut, I freaked. I ran toward them, toward the door, just toward Hawk, to be honest. I didn't have a clue of what to do next. I didn't have a plan of attack, an idea how to fix this. I didn't even have a knife! All I knew was that Hawk was in that room *by himself* with the monster, and that thought alone made everything else secondary.

Ferra saw me move and held me back with one hand. "You can't go out there!" she barked.

"*He's in trouble!*" I screamed as I spun to face her.

"*And you're useless*!" she shouted back at me. Once she had part of my attention, she continued more quietly. "Hawk is a trained warrior. The only thing you can do in there is be a distraction." She picked me up off my feet and tossed me onto my ass behind her. "Stay here with Ruber; I'll tend to the elves." She walked toward the field without looking back. Ruber's dad lowered the barrier to let her pass, and the thought of darting and shadowing her crossed my mind. However, the weak sound of Ruber's voice stopped me.

"Name," he uttered, sounding like a man on his deathbed.

I leaned down closer to the floor. "What?"

"The djinn. If we had its name… we could bind it," he said slowly, each word clearly a massive effort.

"How do we find its name?" I asked, willing him to talk fast, knowing he couldn't, knowing that Hawk was in danger and knowing that Ruber's safety was my responsibility.

"Caerus." He sighed, and I thought he had passed out.

"What? What is that? A place? A book?" I picked him up and resisted the urge to shake him.

"My sister," he whispered, the glow inside of him barely visible.

"She's not a warrior," Adamas interrupted sternly. "She is a lady-in-waiting! Leave her out of this!" Butting into what was clearly an A to B conversation. Which meant he could C his ass out of it.

"I don't care if she's a Malibu Barbie, you freaking rhinestone! If Ruber says she can help, she can help." Though he didn't have a face, I could almost imagine the ugly look the diamond shot at me. I'd been around Ruber long enough to be able to read gem elemental expressions after a fashion. Adamas's scowl was a decent attempt, all things considered. I'd give it an average grade if he was on *Real Housewives*, barely passing as Sue on *Glee*. I guess what I am saying here is when it came to dirty looks, I'd honestly seen better. Of course, the dirty lookers were people. With faces.

"Where is your sister?" I asked Ruber, ignoring King Bedazzled altogether.

"Library," he uttered.

"She wouldn't dare be there!" Adamas said, sounding insulted all over again. "She has no place there!"

"Where we came in," Ruber explained, ignoring his father entirely. "Down that hall to the left."

I stood up, bringing Ruber with me. For a moment I glared at the diamond and thought of the ugliest thing I could say to him. Some doozies came to mind but, for some reason, none of them felt right. Instead, I turned and ran down the hallway, ignoring him completely after that.

"Selene, Rose!" he barked behind me. "Take up the barrier."

I didn't bother to look back, but I knew he was following me.

I am going to be honest. I couldn't have cared less.

FERRA knew the dark elf was dead before she reached him.

There was simply no way any mortal creature could be burnt so badly and live. She knelt down next to Ater, who sat staring at the corpse of his partner. "You need to fall back," Ferra said quietly. "You both do."

He turned his head to look at her, his gaze locking with her own. "I know he's dead. He doesn't need to do anything anymore." And he looked back at his lifemate.

She'd seen this before in members of her own tribe.

It was hard not to fall a little in love with the people you fought beside day in and day out. Though she had no proof, she thought these two might have been closer than that. Ater literally had no reason left to be professional. His unit, his partner, his reason for fighting was dead in front of him, and nothing was going to change that.

"Ater, take your dead and fall back," she said with a bit more emotion. "You can't stay here," she added, looking at the flashes of light that were escaping from the crack under the door. Ater said nothing. "He wouldn't have wanted you to die needlessly."

"You don't know what he would have wanted," the elf hissed in her face.

She drew her hand back and slapped him across the cheek.

The sound echoed in the long hallway, and for a moment she thought he was going to attack her. Instead, one solitary tear escaped his left eye. "Take him and fall back," she repeated quietly as she placed one hand over his. "Look at me! This is more than you and me." She picked up the emerald whose light was barely visible in the dark hall. "You need to get them out of here."

He looked up at her, his eyes red as he struggled not to lose it.

"He will be avenged," she vowed, gripping his hand tightly. "I swear."

He put his other hand over hers and squeezed back and, nodding, he wiped his eyes and picked Pullus up. Ferra laid Lates on Pullus's chest and turned Ater so he'd walk in the right direction. She didn't understand that she'd also put him on a narrow bridge between willing himself to live and willing himself to die, but the Frigus didn't deal with dark elves and knew nothing of them.

Once Ater's uncertain footsteps had faded, she focused again on the door in front of her.

Ferra drew herself up to her full height, taking a deep breath to steady herself.

She placed the palms of her hands on the door and concentrated as hard as she could, calling on every ounce of her being and pouring the concentration into her hands where they touched the door. The door turned light blue instantly before it shattered into splinters as the cold caused it to contract rapidly.

Hawk's body hit her squarely in the chest before she could even lower her arms.

SURE enough, the pink stone that had met us when we teleported in the first time was floating there above a stack of giant jeweled books.

"Father!" she called out in surprise when she noticed Adamas behind me. "Rat—Ruber, what's—oh no!" Ruber pulsed a bit more strongly than he had since he'd come back, mostly to reassure his sister that he still existed.

"What are you doing here?" Adamas roared. The nerve his voice hit was literally my last one.

"*Shut up*!" I screamed as I wheeled to face him. "Just shut your stupid mouth for like ten seconds!"

His expression rated about a B+ on *Housewives* and a full half a Sue from *Glee*.

I spun back to Caerus. "Ruber said if we knew that thing's name, we could bind it or something."

She bobbed for a moment, a gesture I knew was their equivalent of nodding. "It's a djinn, so there are laws it must abide by. However, I have no idea what its name is."

"This is a waste of time! She is a female!" the diamond said, scoffing at her.

I hate scoffing. I mean, if there were an official sound douche bags make, scoffing would be it. I was about to go off on him when Ruber spoke up.

"You said Citrina had left Arcadia as soon as she detected the djinn. Where did it come from?" He sounded stronger, and his color deepened as his energy climbed.

"Oh," she said, sounding a little like Ruber now. "*Oh!* I see what you're getting at!" She took off across the room, knocking over a stack of those tacky-looking Liberace books in her hurry. She used her energies to toss them aside until she found a faded-gold book near the bottom. She aimed a beam of pink light from under her, which activated something in the center of the book's "cover." It lit up like a Christmas tree so I shielded my eyes.

"Citrina said the changeling received a package from the Wolflands from Emperor Fenrir about a year ago...." The light cut off and she flew back toward another corner; the sound of stone books falling to the floor was deafening. "Black Claw was stationed in the Wolflands around that time—where—I know it was—" She was talking more to herself than to us, but no one interrupted her since she was on a roll. "Here it is! He said that the emperor talked about engaging in relations with the changeling, who was acting as an emissary, trading the djinn for favorable terms once the royal family had fallen. Fenrir described the djinn as being spoils of war from the fourth battle of Baghdad." She abandoned the text and flew to another stack of books. "That would mean it would have been originally owned by the Ad-Din dynasty, which means it can be one of two possible names, and since this one has to be contained within larger vessels that would mean it didn't come from the ring, which would make it...."

We all held our breath as she skimmed another book with her freaky light show.

"Udar!" she called out. "It has to be Udar from the lamp. That's its name."

I turned to Bedazzles, all set to see him one scoff and raise him a smug. I was going to be all, "In your face, you overblown piece of glass! *Just a girl*! That gem just went all Willow on your ass and you better respect her, because girls can do anything boys can do except for the peeing standing up thing. Honestly who doesn't want to sit down and read a People magazine while they do their business? If you ask me, girls had it right from the start." Of course, I couldn't say any of that because something smashed into me and yanked out my spleen or kidney or maybe my soul; I wasn't too sure.

So yeah, instead of all that, I just passed out instead.

I'm sure Sparkles got the gist of it anyway.

HAWK brought Truheart up in a mocking salute. "You will deal with me and only me."

The demonic creature's mouth spread out in a leering grin. "I will deal with you the same way I dealt with your whore of a mother."

Hawk's expression didn't flicker as he returned the glare. Only the tone of his voice betrayed his fury. "Can you guess which word in that sentence has earned you a slow and painful death?"

Before the djinn could answer, Hawk launched his attack.

The air between the prince and the creature ignited into flame. Truheart glowed red and absorbed the magical energy, protecting Hawk as he swung at the efreet's face. A fresh cut sliced across its cheek as glowing red liquid that looked more like lava than blood began to flow down toward its chin. Realizing that magical attacks were not going to work, the djinn changed tactics. The fire creature swung its newly formed limb, hitting Hawk in the stomach with the impact of a free-falling boulder. Unprepared for the blow, Hawk went flying, slamming onto and then sliding across the stone floor, stunned. Covering the distance with one stride, the djinn brought down a massive foot with the intention of crushing Hawk where he lay.

Hawk had other ideas. He grasped the sword's hilt and pointed the weapon up and at a slight angle away from himself.

Truheart pierced the sole of the djinn's foot, the tip bursting out the top side as the creature screamed in agony.

Normally Hawk would have taken more time to exploit the wound, but his head still rang from the impact with the floor and he wasn't sure how fast his reflexes were. After a sharp yank on the hilt to increase the angle at which the weapon had stabbed, he left his sword lodged in the djinn's foot and rolled away from the howling beast. Truheart would come at his call when he needed the blade. Taking a second while the elemental tried to pull the sword free, Hawk closed his eyes and focused his energies on healing his wounds. At first he felt nothing. A void echoed where his arcane energies usually resided. He had felt this way after a few intense training sessions, but never so strongly; exhaustion had drained his power before, but never so much. His energies felt as if they were completely gone. He could feel Truheart slip free of the djinn's foot and he knew he didn't have much time. He focused again, pushing farther than he ever had before. He could feel the energy, could almost touch it, but it waited much farther away than he'd ever known it to be.

Drawing upon the power, he cast a spell of regeneration. He felt his body slowly begin to heal itself, the pain and the dizziness fading almost instantly. He saw the efreet balancing Truheart on its palm, finding the center of gravity. Then, in one savage motion, the djinn hurtled the sword at Hawk. Without blinking Hawk clenched his hand and felt the hilt in his grip. Taking a step forward, Hawk threw himself into a spin, building momentum. At the apex of one spin he caught sight of the elemental and launched the sword itself at the monster. The djinn gaped down and saw the blade lodged up to the hilt in its chest. Hawk took a half second to reorient himself before running at the efreet.

The efreet raised one hand and turned the air around Hawk into fire.

Hawk reacted a split second too late to what the djinn had done; the air in the prince's lungs ignited as well. Pure instinct brought Truheart back to his hand, dispelling the magic but not the effects. Focusing on the sword, Hawk increased the power in his regeneration spell. He hadn't been imagining it. Something was resisting him. It was as if the power were actively pulling away from him for some reason. The spell lost speed and began to fracture.

Through sheer force of will, Hawk channeled the spell through Truheart, using the Soul Blade as a conduit, forcing the power to heal him. A wash of cold power swept over and through him as the spell healed the burns all over his body and allowed him to breathe again. Ready to continue the fight, he glared up and caught the efreet's punch in the middle of his face and chest.

He went out like a light as the blow crushed his nose and threw him across the room.

FERRA drew herself up to her full height, taking a deep breath to steady herself.

She placed the palms of her hands on the door and concentrated as hard as she could. The door turned light blue instantly before it shattered into splinters as the cold caused it to contract rapidly.

Hawk's body hit her squarely in the chest before she could even lower her arms.

She caught the unconscious prince reflexively and backed into the hall a few steps until she was able to bobble him into balance. Seeing the efreet charging toward her, she tossed Hawk to the ground and brought her hands up in front of her. The air between her and the efreet began to fog as the temperature dropped first ten, then twenty, then a hundred degrees in seconds. Like a nature film using time lapse photography might show, a lattice of brittle ice that became thicker and thicker with each passing second formed across the doorway.

When the djinn hit it, the sound of hissing steam and a cloud of vapor rose as its skin began to melt the ice wall.

"Ater!" she shouted down the hall. "Get Hawk!"

The dark elf saw the prone figure of the Arcadian heir and ran back to grab him, half dragging him in his need to return to Pullus's side. Ferra focused back on the wall, reinforcing it as the djinn began to actively try to melt it. The heat the efreet generated was impossible to measure, but her people channeled their powers directly from Niflgard, the realm of eternal winter. She could see the djinn's glowing eyes through the ice and the blurred image of its arrogant smile. "This the best you've got?" it asked from the other side of the ice.

At that very instant, she knew it was going to breach the ice wall.

Ferra ignored the outer edges of the wall and focused on its center. Before it could melt entirely, she forged a pillar of ice from the mass and thrust it forward like a battering ram into the djinn before melting. It staggered back as she pressed the attack. Forming a spear in her hand, she brought it low behind the creature's knees, jamming the tip into one set of tendons and slashing them, slamming it to the ground. She stood over it, aiming the spear at its head carefully before plunging it down.

Just as the efreet transformed the air around her to fire as it had with Hawk.

It expected her to scream, to thrash around as the flames consumed her from the inside out. Like Puck had, it assumed her Articus heritage was a weakness when faced with the power of fire. What the djinn learned was the true secret of Ferra's people and the source of their strength. Her skin and hair were burnt away in seconds.

Leaving a sculpture of living ice standing over him.

"*This* is the 'best I got'," she corrected, stabbing it with the ice spear.

The point pierced its skin and steam began to issue out of the breach as she focused her power through the spear to keep it intact. At the site of the wound, the fiery red skin of the djinn began to darken and then slowly turn blue, radiating outward. Its screeches could be heard throughout the entire chamber. "You killed a comrade of mine and seriously injured another tonight," she said through clenched teeth. "Where I come from, that has consequences. Fatal ones." The djinn's entire upper chest had turned blue and its breath had become fog.

"Oh my goodness!" Molly's voice exclaimed from the doorway.

Ferra froze and looked over at her in a panic. "Molly, get out of here!" she shouted before turning back to the efreet.

But she was too late.

Catching Ferra off balance, the djinn bucked the ice warrior off and scrambled to its feet. Knowing it couldn't beat the ice girl on its own merits, it decided to take her out of the fight entirely. It focused its powers on the floor beneath her and it turned to molten rock. She fell into the ground, the lava going up to her neck before it dissipated the heat.

She was literally trapped in the floor.

The efreet turned toward Molly and grinned. "Do you know the melting point of brass?"

Before Molly could answer, Caerus tore around the corner and skidded to a halt, floating above her head. "Nine hundred and thirty degrees Celsius. And your name is Udar."

The creature's body stiffened as it felt the power of its true name pass through it.

Caerus recited a binding spell as the djinn turned and fled back through the dimensional tunnel it had followed the emerald through initially. Adamas and Ruber rounded the corner just in time to see the djinn vanish into the ground, the pink sapphire hot on its tail. In a panic, the diamond called after his daughter to stop.

She paused at the tunnel's entry point and hovered above the portal.

"You want to travel through the earth so badly?" she said out loud. "Then stay down there!" She glowed brightly as she cast a Dispel ward over the aperture. The dimensional tunnel began to collapse behind the efreet as it raced across the realms. It looked back just in time to see the earth behind it solidify around it. It had time for part of a scream before it was frozen into the rock.

Caerus floated up and looked back at her father. "It won't be coming back."

Before the king could answer, Molly cried out, "She's still in the floor! *Do something*!"

Shocked, all three gems gazed at the encased warrior. She said in a weak voice, “Some assistance?”

Adamas and Ruber began the delicate task of freeing Ferra without harming her, as Molly looked on, speaking quietly to Ferra to distract her.

CHAPTER THIRTEEN

"There is no happily ever after.
There is just not miserable for now."
Carabosse

WHEN Hawk woke up, Ruber was floating next to his bed.

"Where's Kane?" was his first question, which didn't seem to surprise the ruby at all.

"Still unconscious," Ruber explained as he floated toward the bed next to Hawk's. Kane lay there, barely breathing, his skin a sickly white that made him look like a corpse.

"What happened to him?" Hawk asked, sitting up and shakily tossing his covers back.

Ruber paused for a moment, trying to find a diplomatic way of conveying the problem. Coming to the conclusion that there was no polite way, he finally just said, "You did."

Hawk's eyes widened in shock as he knelt down. Kane's hand was cold and lifeless and seemed so small clasped between his own. "What did I do?"

"You died," Ruber answered, openly filled with sorrow. "The nyxies had inflicted too much damage on your body in The Under. When we found you on the altar, it was already too late."

Hawk looked up at the rock, eyes wide with confusion. "But I'm here."

"Because he plunged Truheart into your chest," Ruber replied cryptically.

Hawk's fingers traced his chest; a phantom echo of the blow was still there. "That wouldn't do anything, though."

"This time it did. He freely shared his soul with you."

The words should have shocked the prince into denial, but for some reason he knew they were true. He hadn't had words for it and had thought the increased bond was The Calling, but deep down he'd known it was something else.

"You are both sharing one soul, which would have been acceptable if you were allowed time to heal properly."

Hawk whispered, "The spell didn't heal me."

"No," Ruber said solemnly. "Kane did. It was his life force that kept you alive until your own could repair enough to stand with it."

"Fix him," Hawk ordered, standing up.

"There is nothing wrong with him physically. He simply doesn't have enough life force to keep going." Ruber added with a catch in his voice, "Hawk, he's dying."

"No," the prince said, turning back to Kane's body. "No he isn't."

"There is nothing you can do," Ruber warned him.

"You're wrong," Hawk said, kneeling next to Kane "There is a power greater than death." He leaned over and slid one arm around Kane's shoulders, gathered him as close as possible, and rested his forehead against Kane's.

"And that is?" Ruber asked skeptically.

Ruber's question came from far away and Hawk answered absently, a bit surprised the gem didn't already know. He held his breath as he looked down at Kane, his entire life passing before his eyes. As he leaned forward, he could feel every second before this one become irrelevant. His lips inches away from Kane's, he whispered one word as his answer.

"Love."

And Hawk kissed him. The cold lips beneath his remained still, but Hawk didn't falter. Every atom of his being cajoled Kane's life force to return, to creep out from the safe places where it had hidden. The thoughts he shared, the words his mind sent to the silent young man, Hawk never mentioned afterward. Letting everything in his heart and soul go, he surrendered it all to Kane. When his soul touched the human's, the two collided, and a wash of love swept across and around and through the room and those in it.

Across the cavern, Ater sat by the corpse of his partner and silently watched. He could not imagine a life without Pullus, which was not true because he *could* imagine it. He just didn't want to live it. He was in the darkest place he had ever known. Then he felt *it.* The desolate feeling that had descended on him since his mate's death faded as he felt the echo of his own love flare back into his heart.

Quietly he began to cry.

Ferra sat next to Molly, trying to answer the clockwork companion's limitless questions about her new state. The warrior was self-conscious about her icy appearance, but the brass girl seemed to be so taken by it that she couldn't help but smile. She was unsure what to say. The Elders had been quite clear on what Logos felt about unnatural love and the consequences for speaking of it out loud. She had spent her life trying to atone for that one sin, trying to beg forgiveness.

It hit her like a wave of heat, dispelling all her doubts and fears. She leaned forward and kissed Molly passionately. Luckily, Molly's Coquette spring was still tight, so she kissed back.

Caerus had settled on Lates's sleep surface, keeping him company as he recovered from his ordeal. The younger emerald's color was lighter. If he had been human the equivalent would have been a streak of white hair, indicating a recent terror. She was reciting a story she remembered their mother telling her and Ruber in the distant past when Adamas floated in.

Father and daughter hadn't talked since the battle, and she knew she couldn't gauge how he was going to react to her actions in the library.

"Father," she said in a respectful tone.

"How is he?" the diamond asked, floating closer to his children.

"Weak, but getting stronger," she reported dutifully.

"That was a very brave thing you did, Lates," Adamas said to his youngest.

"Thank you, sire."

"Do not ever think of doing it again." Adamas's tone might have convinced others that he had spoken in jest, but the emerald knew his father was not joking.

"Yes, sir," he answered meekly.

"As for you—" Adamas said to the sapphire.

Caerus steeled herself for the lecture.

They both felt *it* pass over them.

"You were incredible," Adamas said, the awe in his voice unmistakable. "Your mother would have been so proud of you."

The glow inside of her brightened as she blushed from the compliment. "You're not angry?"

"I'm furious," he said with not a trace of anger in his voice. "But that doesn't mean I don't want my daughter to be happy. Does being in there make you happy?" he asked, openly curious.

"Very much so," she said quietly.

"Then I suppose we have a new keeper of the stories," he declared proudly as he floated out of the room.

"What was that?" Lates asked when they were alone.

"Love," she said, completely floored by her father's reaction.

Ruber watched as Kane's eyes fluttered open, his hands moving around Hawk's free hand automatically. The color came back to his cheeks as he kissed Hawk back. The transformation was as astonishing as it was impossible. The gem had never seen such a humble but blindingly complete display of power before.

Kane smiled as he pulled back three microns from the kiss. "You saved me," he said breathlessly.

“I was saving myself,” Hawk said, gazing into his true love’s eyes. “There is simply no way I could exist without you.

“It’s always about you, isn’t it?” Kane asked, smiling.

Hawk smiled back. “It’s a little bit about you.”

“You’re… you’re mine now, aren’t you?” Kane asked, the thoughts crammed in his head not translating to words as easily as he thought they would.

Hawk nodded with a smile. “We are karus.”

Kane had a vague understanding that the word meant they were joined or together now, but the fine details escaped him.

“What the hell was that?” Ruber asked, sounding almost outraged.

Hawk looked up, still holding Kane close. “That, my finely faceted friend, was the power of true love.” He looked back to Kane, who was blushing now. “There is nothing more powerful in the nine realms.”

“Love? That, all of this, was from a simple emotion?” Ruber asked, obviously not believing it.

Hawk had gone back to looking at Kane. “There is nothing simple about it.”

Ruber floated away, disgusted. If the prince wasn’t going to tell him how he had healed Kane, there was no reason for him to make up stories about it.

SO a couple of days later, Hawk called us all together.

Ferra was there with her new robot girlfriend. The two of them had been pretty lovey-dovey, which was okay with me, since I was still floating from Hawk’s kiss and declaration of love and we’d been pretty lovey-dovey ourselves. Ferra looked badass in her new ice form, even though she seemed to be kind of embarrassed by it.

Ater stood off in the corner. There was a darkness around him now that made my heart ache. I had known he and Pullus had been a couple but I honestly didn't think it was that serious, but looking at the way he was hurting now, I felt stupid for not seeing it before. He tried not to stare at Hawk and me when we were together. I think our closeness made him feel even worse.

Ruber and his sister were there. She was all Hermione in her new job and had sent an agent to Arcadia to look in on Hawk's parents. The diamond had done a one-eighty on us; I'm pretty sure Hawk saving his youngest son had something to do with that. We had gone from a pack of hillbilly intruders to valued guests overnight.

"Tell them what you told me," Hawk said to Caerus once everyone had found a place to sit or float.

"The Arcadian royal family has been ousted by Puck. He has taken control of the capital and has declared martial law across the land. He has armies of the Dark moving out from the capital. There are rumors that he is forcing the governors to either pledge allegiance or be killed. I have reports of pillaging in at least three towns." She paused and I saw Hawk nod, prompting her to continue.

"There has been a public declaration that Titania will be executed by the end of the summer solstice. She is to be executed for crimes against the Dark."

Ater pushed off of the wall. "It's a trap."

Hawk nodded to him. "I know."

Molly stared around at everyone. "A trap for what?"

"For me," Hawk said, anger in his voice. "Puck is using her as bait to capture me."

Ferra looked confused. "Why? He has the capital. Why does he need you?"

Hawk sighed and stood up. He unbuttoned his shirt and pulled out the gold chain around his neck. As soon as he pulled the chain free of his shirt, a golden acorn appeared on the chain. I was kinda shocked, since I had, um, experienced Hawk with his shirt off and had never once seen the pendant before. "This is the secret to Ascension."

"A seed?" Ater asked, obviously not expecting *that* to be the secret.

"Of course," Caerus said before Hawk could answer. "That makes sense."

"It does?" Ruber asked, looking at her.

"That's a seed to the next world tree, isn't it?" she asked, floating closer to Hawk.

"It is—the last one."

"World tree?" I asked, completely lost.

"The nine realms are said to be supported by a huge tree, each world being part of it from the roots to the crown. Without the tree, the realms would have no connection," Caerus explained and then asked Hawk, "And this is the last one?"

Hawk buttoned his shirt and put the chain back. The acorn vanished, not even leaving a lump where it lay. "Wherever the seed is planted will become the center of the nine realms, and whoever plants it becomes their ruler."

"So even if Puck kills your mother, he still can't Ascend until he has that?" Ater asked.

Hawk nodded. "It's why I was sent to Earth, where Mother thought it couldn't fall into the wrong hands."

"Does Puck know about the seed?" Ferra asked.

Ater shook his head. "No, but he knows there is a trick to Ascending. If he finds out about the seed…." He trailed off, knowing everyone could figure out what would happen.

"So then we keep it from him," Ferra reasoned. "Case closed."

"No," Hawk barked, openly angry for the first time. "He has my mother."

"Your mother is bait," Ater warned. "There is no way we can take the capital back."

Hawk nodded. "There is no way those of us in this room can take the capital, I agree. But I am not allowing that bastard changeling to harm a hair on my mother's head."

"So then what?" Ater demanded.

"We need an army," I said, thinking out loud.

"We need an army," Hawk said, giving me a grim smile.

No one talked for almost a minute.

Finally, Ferra clapped her hands, rubbing them together. "Okay, then. Where do we find an army?"

THE STUFF THAT IS AFTER THE BOOK

I REMEMBER growing up that some of the best parts of the books I read were the stuff that came after the story was done. Piers Anthony's *Xanth* series comes to mind. I remember loving the parts where he just talked about his life and the process of writing the book almost as much as the book itself. It's funny, though, because now that I sit here and write this, I wonder how self-indulgent I'm really being. In this digital age of instant blogging, we have become almost numb to the concept of reading the inner thoughts and feelings of other people and forget how precious they can be.

This book owes its existence to a process, much like the way Ruber's people do. Stories have a way of instilling themselves into our lives, becoming so much a part of our tapestries that it's impossible to remember the time before we read them. *Neverwhere* by Neil Gaiman is like that for me. I remember, in the month or so after reading it, looking into the shadows, wondering if I could see that other world I *knew* was just next to ours. So there are a thousand other stories that have given their energy to create this one, and I hope this one sparks a thousand more. There are always other stories to be told, even if at their core they are all the same.

I am owned by three cats, two black and one dumb one. Now the dumb one is an adorable cat who knows just how pretty he is, because if he wasn't there would, of course, be no reason for me not to pitch him out of the house on a daily basis. His name is Samuel Sora Bartholomew Bunny (Sammy to his friends), and he has a very simple way of looking at life. There are the things he wants, the things he does not want, and the things that pet him. He is very set in his ways, and any attempt to alter his behavior inevitably ends up with him giving me a look that can only be translated as "Why are you killing me?" I love him dearly; again, if I didn't, there would be no reason to tolerate his never-ending series of demands.

The smaller black cat is called Baby Faith. I say called because I am not sure what her name is; she simply responds to that one because it suits her. She does not live in my house; she is a prisoner of war. I know this because of the way she eyes the silverware when she thinks I'm not looking. I am not her dad, her owner, or her friend. I am the management of the place she is forced to occupy right now. Which means my duties are to replace the contents of the complementary crunchy bowl every day, to make sure there is a supply of fresh water whenever she so wishes it, to provide her uninterrupted time on the veranda (through the sliding glass door in my room) when she books it, and nothing more. I am not to attempt to put my hands on her for any monkey business like pettings or other displays of affection. She is constantly reminding me of my place in our relationship. She stays in the house because, frankly, I am simply too scared to try to kick her out.

And then there is my cat, Little Eddie.

By the way, these names make little sense to people who are not me or my close friends. There is no Adult Faith, unless you count the kickass slayer from *Buffy*, nor is there a Big Eddie, unless you are referencing Jensen Ackles's little-known series called *Slayers,* where he played a telepathic dream named Eddie. Please do not rush to IMDb to look that up, by the way. It doesn't exist.

Anyway, Little Eddie is my cat. No, that's not right. I am not his human either; that kind of relationship would mean one of us has authority over the other one, and that's not how we roll. If anything, we are equals in life. I provide him with food, water, and affection, and he provides me with the great joy of supplying these things to him. He is always close to me, but never on me. He is aware of where I am at all times, but never hovers. He is a lot like me in the fact that neither one of us have a great affection for people who are not us, and we cover that with a general disdain that is impossible to miss. He is the only cat I can actually claim, since Faith is simply biding her time until she learns how to handle a knife without thumbs, and Sammy, much like a goldfish, is surprised to meet me every time I enter the room. Eddie is mine and I am his. It's really the only way it works, and we're both okay with that.

What does this have to do with anything?

Well, my point is this. A cat is a cat is a cat the same way a story is a story is a story. Anyone can say every story has already been told, but unless you read that new story, you will never know how wrong you are. Each story is its own person who walks and talks, and if you're a reader, that story becomes a friend and a companion. Even though you have other friends, each one is unique. I know writers who lose focus because they are afraid of writing what other people have covered. To them, I say this: do you avoid people with black hair because you already have a black-haired friend?

If you want to be a writer, the trick isn't learning how to write, it is learning how to tell a story. Anyone can write. Anyone. You can write a grocery list, you can write directions to the store, and you can even write the recipe for the dish you're working on. The challenge is telling a story. A lot of people get caught up in the specifics, even though when they are face-to-face with someone, they don't worry about misspeaking or getting it wrong. They open their mouths without fear of being corrected, and they just talk. The human brain is a wonderful thing; it can make sense of just about anything if you give it enough time.

My suggestion, if you want to write, is that you find someone who knows the rules. And by the rules I mean, of course, the English language. Someone who gets where things are supposed to go in a sentence so that it doesn't sound like you are a gray tabby who is just blown away by how many people live in his house, since he has never run into the same guy twice.

My someone is Gayle. When I say the things you are reading right now make sense because of her, I cannot stress how much that is true. Besides being wildly supportive, she has everything a writer needs: patience, honesty, and a love of plurals without apostrophes. If you can find a Gayle, hold on to her with both hands and never let go; she'll change your life. It also helps if she is a good friend too. Makes the whole process flow.

Find a group of people who will read your crap unedited. This is going to take some time. I have Gina, who will read my stuff no matter how bad it is and will sift through it to find the small specks of gold that may be contained within the mass of chaos I send her. But don't just find people who will read, find people who will read and be honest with you. I have a Tom and a Debbie for that as well. Though they are fans of what I write, they also know I want them to say, "Wow, so you know the parts where you put the words together? Yeah, don't do it like that anymore."

These people are also worth their weight in gold, and if you can find them, never let them go.

You know what also helps? Knowing people who have actually written stuff before and who hold a gun to your head while they shout at you that you need to publish stuff. For that I have a Sue and, though I am pretty sure she was just being nice at first, she is the *only* reason you are reading this at all. When you find people like that, never stop thanking them. Seriously. Never stop.

Thank you, Sue.

Now, those are the individual components you will need to help you as you write. However, if you don't *do* something, nothing will happen. If you do not write and let people read what you've written, you will never be a writer.

I have—I almost said *had,* but that would be lying—I have a crippling fear of having other people read my words. In the course of writing these paragraphs, I have contemplated deleting them about a dozen times. But I figured, hey, you bought the story and read it. If you didn't like the story, you aren't going to like this. Which means the only people reading this had to have liked something about the story enough to keep reading after it ended.

By the way, thank you for that too.

I joined a blogging site and began writing, dreading the moment when someone might read what I'd written. And people did. Some loved my stuff, others didn't, and most gave me a thumbs-up for the effort. What blogging did was prove to my fear that just because I wrote something and someone didn't like it, the world would not stop and my heart would not burst. Eventually, I would write again. People will not like what you write. Count on it. Name a book, any book, and I will find a dozen people who don't like it. Does it make it a bad book? No. It just means they didn't like it. There is a ton of stuff other people do that I don't like that continues to exist (much to my displeasure) and, in fact, thrives. My opinion is only one of many. No matter how different your words may be, someone will like them.

But that's not the point.

I don't need to like your writing. Sue doesn't need to like your writing. Gayle will probably say she likes it, but she is really, really nice so she doesn't count. None of us have to love your writing.

You do.

That's it. That's the man behind the curtain. (Seriously, I said "no damn dogs in the throne room!" This is why I'm a cat person. Know what would have happened if Dorothy had brought Little Eddie with her instead of Toto? Well, no, that's a bad example because Little Eddie would have slapped her silly for letting the ugly woman with the bicycle take him, then he would have tackled the bicycle lady to the ground, taken her bike, and pedaled off to find me. The point is, if Dorothy had brought a cat, a non-Eddie cat, the cat would have known the entire time that an old man stood behind the curtain, running things. The cat would then have cut a deal with the old guy for two bowls of tuna and some good neck scratches. His silence could be bought on the daily installment plan for the rest of his life.)

Where was I?

Oh right, *you* have to like your writing. If you don't, then stop writing. You can be dissatisfied with the level of your ability, you can marvel at other authors' ways of making word art, but if you honestly read your stuff and cannot imagine a reason for someone else to read it, neither will anyone else.

All writers have to possess a terrible sort of arrogance about their writing, and that arrogance has to be owned by the writer. We are forging worlds of our own creation; then we are trying to make you see them. The process is not a democracy or a committee. What I write literally creates the way I want my world to be. If you read it, you have to believe the way I've written my world too. If a writer doesn't have absolute certainty about his or her words, why should anyone else?

Writers don't write because they are bored. True writers write because they don't know how *not* to write. They have words that *must* be shared with others, stories that demand to be told. If you can't find that passion, that desire to create them, then, my friend, you have failed before you have begun. However, if you do have that passion and you do think your words are worth reading, if you have the courage to have others read them and you find people who will help you craft your words and stories….

Well, then, you are only three cats shy of being a writer.

SO there is going to be some confusion about the quotes that are before each chapter. Some sound familiar, I am sure; some sound completely postal. They are all clues to the nature of the nine realms. Most are said by a very specific character; some you may already know.

I know Max is out there right now scrambling to Wikipedia and Google to suss it all out.

I don't want anyone to feel pressured to have to do homework to figure them out. They are not necessary to enjoy the book at all. You can take them at face value and live the rest of your life not knowing the identities of who said what. But for those of you who like to dig….

I would suggest using other languages as your starting point. Latin and French, to be more specific. Also remember that I am referring to fictional characters, so if your investigation leads you to a real-life person, you might have gone too far. Finally, remember that each of the nine realms is specific in its population; just as Ruber's land is populated by gem elementals and Dwarves, the other realms are equally specific.

Again, I assume you wouldn't have read this far if you hadn't liked the book. I am just offering you a clue that there is always more to a story.

Good hunting!

John Goode

May 2012

Just East of Neverland

(The land, not the ranch. Just saying.)

JOHN GOODE is a member of the class of '88 from Hogwarts School of Witchcraft and Wizardry, specializing in incantations and spoken spells. At the age of fourteen, he proudly represented District 13 in the 65th Panem games, where he was disqualified for crying uncontrollably before the competition began. After that he moved to Forks, Washington, where against all odds he dated the hot, incredibly approachable werewolf instead of the stuck-up jerk of a vampire, but was crushed when he found out the werewolf was actually gayer than he was. After that he turned down the mandatory operation everyone must receive at sixteen to become pretty, citing that everyone pretty was just too stupid to live, before moving away for greener pastures. After falling down an oddly large rabbit hole, he became huge when his love for cakes combined with his inability to resist the commands of sparsely worded notes, and was finally kicked out when he began playing solitaire with the Red Queen's 4th armored division. By eighteen he had found the land in the back of his wardrobe, but decided that thinly veiled religious allegories were not the neighbors he desired. When last seen, he had become obsessed with growing a pair of wings after discovering Fang's blog and hasn't been seen since.

Or he is this guy who lives in this place and writes stuff he hopes you read.

Also by JOHN GOODE

http://www.harmonyinkpress.com

Harmony Ink

CPSIA information can be obtained at www.ICGtesting.com
Printed in the USA
LVOW130723290912

300809LV00001B/2/P